The Golden Dog Book
of
Fairy Tales
and
Animal Stories

The Golden Dog Book

of

Fairy Tales

and

Animal Stories

Edited by
Robert B. Lovejoy

The Golden Dog Press
Ottawa – Canada – 1996

Copyright © 1996 Introduction, editorial emendations and image by Robert B. Lovejoy and The Golden Dog Press.

ISBN 0-919614-66-3 (paperback)

Canadian Cataloguing in Publication Data
Main entry under title:
    The Golden Dog book of fairy tales and animal stories

Includes bibliographical references.

ISBN 0-919614-66-3

    1. Fairy tales.   2. Animals–Fiction.   3. Animals–Folklore.   I. Lovejoy, R.B.
(Robert Barton), 1937–

PZ8.G64 1996   398.2   C96-900403-6

Cover design by The Gordon Creative Group of Ottawa.

Text layout by Ch. Thiele, Carleton Production Centre of Nepean.

Printed in Canada by AGMV "l'imprimeur" Inc., of Cap-Saint-Ignace, Québec.

Distributed by:

    Oxford University Press Canada,
    70 Wynford Drive, DON MILLS, Ont., Canada, M3C 1J9.
    Phone: 416-441-2941   *   Fax: 416-444-0427

The Golden Dog Press wishes to express its appreciation to the Canada Council and the Ontario Arts Council for current and past support of its publishing programme.

Contents

Introduction
Robert B. Lovejoy

For many readers of this collection, the world of fairy tales will seem quite alien. Our culture associates the "fairy tale" with wonderful magic and glittering princesses, fairy godmothers and glass slippers. For example, one edition of Andrew Lang's famous *Blue Fairy Book* (1889) entices the reader to enter this stereotypical world of marvel and romance: "Here in this wonderful collection of fairy tales are stories that children all over the world have come to love. You can wander through the forest with Little Red Riding Hood on her way to Grandma's house, puzzle with the pretty princess as she tries to guess the riddle of Rumplestilzkin's strange and funny name, or enjoy the much-told tale of the ragged, but beautiful Cinderella and how she got to the Prince's ball" (5). The tone here suggests that fairy tales are easily read and casually digested, but how far from the truth of fairy tales this is. Red Riding Hood may "wander" through the forest, but does her innocence deserve the devouring wolf she finds at grandma's house? The "pretty princess" of *Rumplestilzkin* has been bargained away by a father's desire to impress a king and grow rich, and further, she has had to bargain away her first-born to save her own life. These are not pretty, or magical, or wondrous situations.

Fairy tales present us with a world where only heroic effort and luck and magical intervention can save the innocent and good from an almost overwhelming power of evil. These stories were not written or told solely for the delight of children, but for listeners of all ages. The development of a literature intended for the child reader from the 16th through the 19th centuries meant that fairy tales were to be revised and adapted for the young listener and reader. Certainly such tales appeal strongly to children because most of the heroes are children who are often mistreated by a parent or step-parent, or older brothers and sisters, but who struggle and usually triumph. Fairy tales are essentially the "hero" story, the sort of story that appeals to all of us, whether the tale is of David and Goliath or Beauty and the Beast. These are the sorts of tales that as Bruno Bettelheim says provide "consolation ... the greatest service the fairy tale can offer a child: the confidence that, despite all tribulation he has to suffer (such as the threat of desertion by parents in 'Hansel and Gretel'; jealousy on the part of parents in 'Snow White' and of siblings in 'Cinderella' ...) not only will he succeed, but the evil forces will be done away with and never again threatened his peace of mind" (147).

But who wrote these strange tales? Readers often think that the Grimms and Perrault and Andersen did; however, we can be quite sure that these three famous tellers depended upon a long-standing oral tradition, filled with powerful stories. Jacob and Wilhelm Grimm were collectors of old tales, not original tellers. They defined their role as scribes, aiming to give us exact written recreations of stories told them by their informants. However, the most recent scholarship on the Grimm brothers shows us they went far beyond exact retellings (see Ellis and Tatar), often revising in order to heighten the "morality" or lesson of the stories. Perrault and Andersen were clearly more than editors or collectors. They were conscious creators of their own stories and styles. Yet, they relied upon the oral tradition for the sources of most of their tales. Thus an answer to "who wrote these tales?" must be found in the rich collaboration of oral tellers and literary adaptors.

Perhaps the most interesting question about fairy tales is how should we read them, what should the reader look for, and can the often strange, even bizarre events that go into fairy tales be accounted for in some way? To my mind there are two versions of how to read these tales that should be examined: Bruno Bettelheim's *The Uses of Enchantment* and Anne Wilson's *The Traditional Story*. Other scholars have examined fairy tales with much care: Propp, Zipes, Sale, Lüthi (see the "Selected Texts"), but only Wilson and Bettelheim create extended arguments on the way tales should be read. Briefly, they share certain conclusions about the way to approach fairy tales: 1) both believe in the intense identification established between reader and hero in each tale, 2) both try to account for the elaboration of detail in the stories and to "make sense" of the apparent arbitrariness of this detail, and 3) both argue that the "explanation" for the tales resides "inside" the reader. Wilson, a scholar of medieval romance, links her interpretation of these stories to an understanding of dream and the symbolic work of dreams; Bettelheim, a children's psychoanalyst, links his "reading" to Freudian theory of the child's psycho-sexual development (e.g. oral greed in "Hansel and Grettel"). Although both Bettelheim and Wilson acknowledge that fairy tales were not solely written for the child reader, they argue that the tales offer a child a particularly intense and valuable experience. For Wilson this experience derives from the "total identification" of child reader with the story hero; for Bettelheim, the stories re-create deep, unconscious conflicts in the child and offer a realization that through effort and struggle, the child can grow beyond these conflicts. Both of these interpretations of what the child finds at work in fairy tales deserve careful study, especially Wilson's book which is more a literary analysis than Bettelheim's.

However, this collection contains more than just the fairy tales. The aim here also is to include some rightfully famous stories that link to both fairy and folk tale. The stories by Harris, Thompson Seton, and Kipling are intended to represent some of the best of the tradition of animal stories and the trickster hero. Few people read the Brer Rabbit tales anymore, but they should be read—and read aloud. The dialect poses some small problems, but if read aloud the difficulty lasts only for a few sentences. Once into a story of Brers Rabbit, Fox and Bear, it's hard to stop. Brer Rabbit, the finest of trickster heroes, takes his turn in the line from "Puss in Boots", through Riki Tiki Tavi, to such figures as Hazel in *Watership Down* and E.B. White's Charlotte. Perhaps these are the sorts of heroes the child reader enjoys most: the small and wily and clever stretching brain and nerve to meet dangers eye to eye and never blink, but responding to pressure by buying bits of time until some plan, or the next step toward some plan, emerges. This is the stuff of great drama, of tense action, and of telling wit. "Bred en bawn in a briar-patch, Brer Fox—bred en bawn in a briar patch!" is the sort of line every child should know and carry as a lucky charm in a deep pocket somewhere within. Not to have this magical boast of Brer Rabbit's deposited within a child's "inner" ear means the adult guide has failed just that much. If nothing else, I hope this collection means a few more children will hear that ringing, even jangling, moment of Brer Rabbit's triumphant scorn.

One small matter more—collections always create the difficulty of providing too much to read because the reader usually insists on pushing on from one story to the next relentlessly. These tales and stories ought to be read unhurriedly, one after another, with long pauses of separation between them. Take time to absorb the language of each story and re-read until the tales that you like best become part of you, so that for you they can become touched a bit with permanence.

The Frog Prince
Jakob and Wilhelm Grimm

In olden times, when people could have all they wished for at once, lived a king who had many beautiful daughters; but the youngest was so lovely that the sun himself would wonder whenever he shone on her face. Near to the king's castle lay a dark, gloomy forest, in the midst of which stood an old linden tree, shading with its foliage the pleasant waters of a fountain.

One day, when the weather was very hot, the king's daughter came into the forest, and seated herself on the side of the cool fountain, and when at last the silence became wearisome, she began to toss a golden ball in the air, and catch it again, as an amusement. Presently, however, the king's daughter failed to catch the golden ball in her hand, so that it fell on the ground, and rolled over the grass into the water.

The princess followed it with her eyes till it disappeared, for the water was so deep that she could not see the bottom.

Then she cried aloud, and began to weep bitterly for the loss of her golden ball. Presently she heard a voice exclaiming:

"Why do you weep, O king's daughter? Your tears could melt even the stones to pity you."

She looked at the spot from whence the voice came, and saw a frog stretching his thick ugly head out of the water.

"Oh, there you are, old water-paddler!" she said. "Well, then, I am crying for the loss of my golden ball that has fallen into the fountain."

"Then weep no more," answered the frog; "I can get it for you. But what will you give me if I fetch your plaything?"

"Oh, anything you like, dear frog!" she replied. "What will you have — my dresses, my pearls and jewels, or the golden crown I wear sometimes?"

"Neither," answered the frog. "Your clothes, your pearls, and your jewels, or even your golden crown, are nothing to me. I want you to love me, and let me be your companion and playfellow. I should like to sit at your table, eat from your golden plate and drink out of your cup, and sleep in your nice little bed. If you will promise me all this, then I will dive down into the water and bring up your pretty golden ball."

"Oh, yes" she replied. "I will promise you anything you like if you will only bring up my ball again."

But she thought to herself that a silly, chattering frog as he was, living in the water with others like himself, and croaking, could not be fit to associate with mankind.

The frog, who believed in the promise of the king's daughter, dipped his head under the water, and sank down to the bottom, where he quickly found the ball, and seizing it in his mouth, carried it to the surface and threw it on the grass. When the king's daughter saw the beautiful play-thing, she was full of joy, and, catching it up, ran away as fast as she could run.

"Wait, wait!" cried the frog, "take me with you; I cannot run so fast as you can!" But the young princess would not listen to the frog's croaking; she got to the house as fast as she could, and soon forgot the poor frog, who was obliged to return to the fountain and remain there.

The next day, however, while the princess was sitting with the king and his courtiers, and eating out of her own little golden plate, she heard a strange noise on the marble steps outside, splish, splash, splish, splash, and presently came a knock at the door, and a voice cried: "Lovely princess, open the door for me." So she rose and went to see who could be outside; but when she caught sight of the frog, she closed the door hastily and seated herself again at the table, looking quite pale. The king, seeing that his daughter was alarmed, said to her: "My child, what is there at the door? Is it a giant come to carry you away?"

"Oh, no, my father!" she replied. "It is no giant, only a great ugly frog."

"A frog! What can he want with you, my daughter?"

"Ah, my dear father, I will tell you all about it. Yesterday, when I was playing with my golden ball by the fountain in the forest, I let it fall into the water, and because I cried, the frog fetched it out for me, and he made me promise that he should come to the castle and be my companion, for I thought he could not get out of the water to come to me, and now here he is."

Just then came a second knock at the door, and a voice cried:

"King's daughter, king's daughter, open for me!

You promised that I your companion should be, When you sat in the shade from the sun's bright beam, And I fetched up your ball from the fountain's cool stream."

"Then," said the king, "my daughter, you must keep your promise; go and let him in at once." So she was obliged to go and open the door, and the frog hopped in after her close to her feet and quite up to her chair. But when she sat down he cried: "Take me up by you." She would not at first, till her father obliged her to lift the frog on the chair by her side. He was no sooner there than he jumped upon the table and said: "Now, then, push your little golden plate nearer, and we will eat together."

The princess did as he told her, but every one could see how much she disliked it. The frog seemed to relish his dinner very much, but he would give the princess half of all he took. At last he said: "I have eaten and drunk quite enough, and I feel very tired, so now carry me upstairs into your little bedroom, and make your silken bed ready, that we may sleep together."

When the princess heard this, she began to weep, for she was really afraid of the cold frog: she could not even touch him, and now he actually wanted to sleep in her neat, beautiful little bed.

But the king was displeased at her tears, and he said: "He who helped you when you were in trouble must not be despised now." So the young princess found she must obey. Then she took up the frog with two fingers, and holding him as far from her as possible, she carried him upstairs and placed him in a corner of her room.

In the evening, however, as soon as the princess was in bed, the frog crept out of his corner and said to her: "I am so tired; lift me up and let me sleep in your bed, or I will tell your father."

On hearing this the princess fell into a great passion, so seizing the frog in her hand, she dashed him with all her strength against the wall, saying: "You will be quiet now, I hope, you ugly frog."

But as he fell, how surprised she was to see the frog change into a handsome young prince, with beautiful friendly eyes, who afterward became her constant companion, and at last her father gave his consent to their marriage.

Before it took place, however, the prince told them his history, how he had been changed into a frog by a wicked witch, and that she had condemned him to live in the fountain until a king's daughter should come and release him. No one else in the world had the power to do so. After they were married, the young prince proposed that he should take his bride to his own kingdom. So on the wedding-day a splendid carriage drawn by eight white horses drove up to the door. They had white feathers on their heads and golden harnesses, and by the side of the carriage stood the prince's steward, the faithful Harry. This faithful Harry had been so unhappy when his master was changed into a frog that he had fastened three iron bands round his heart, to prevent it from bursting with woe and sorrow.

The carriage with the prince and his bride soon drove away, with Harry behind in his old place, and full of joy at the release of his master. They had not traveled far when they heard a loud crack — as if something had broken. Now, the prince knew nothing of the iron bands round his servant's heart, so he cried out: "Harry, is the carriage breaking?"

"No, sire," he replied, "only the iron bands which I bound round my heart for fear it should burst with sorrow while you were a frog confined to the fountain. They are breaking now because I am so happy to see my master restored to his own shape, and traveling to his kingdom with a beautiful bride."

The prince and princess never forgot faithful Harry, who had loved his master so well while he was in trouble.

Hansel and Grethel
Jakob and Wilhelm Grimm

Near the borders of a large forest dwelt in olden times a poor woodcutter who had two children—a boy named Hansel, and his sister, Grethel. They had very little to live upon and once, when there was a dreadful season of scarcity in the land, the poor woodcutter could not earn sufficient to supply their daily food.

One evening, after the children were gone to bed, the parents sat talking together over their sorrow, and the poor husband sighed, and said to his wife, who was not the mother of his children, but their stepmother: "What will become of us, for I cannot earn enough to support myself and you, much less the children? What shall we do with them? for they must not starve."

"I know what to do, husband," she replied. "Early to-morrow morning we will take the children for a walk across the forest and leave them in the thickest part; they will never find the way home again, you may depend, and then we shall only have to work for ourselves."

"No, wife," said the man, "that I will never do; how could I have the heart to leave my children all alone in the wood, where the wild beasts would come quickly and devour them?"

"Oh, you fool!" replied the stepmother; "if you refuse to do this, you know we must all four perish with hunger; you may as well go and cut the wood for our coffins." And after this she let him have no peace till he became quite worn out, and could not sleep for hours, but lay thinking in sorrow about his children.

The two children, who also were too hungry to sleep, heard all that their stepmother had said to their father. Poor little Grethel wept bitter tears as she listened, and said to her brother, "What is going to happen to us, Hansel?"

"Hush, Grethel," he whispered; "don't be so unhappy; I know what to do."

Then they lay quite still till their parents were asleep.

As soon as it was quiet Hansel got up, put on his little coat, unfastened the door, and slipped out. The moon shone brightly, and the white pebble stones which lay before the cottage door glistened like new silver money. Hansel stooped and picked up as many of the pebbles as he could stuff in his little coat pockets. He then went back to Grethel and said: "Be comforted, dear litlte sister,and sleep in peace; Heaven will take care of us." Then he laid himself down again in bed and slept till the day broke.

As soon as the sun was risen the stepmother came and woke the two children, and said: "Get up, you lazybones, and come into the wood with me to gather wood for the fire." Then she gave each of them a piece of bread, and said: "You must keep that to eat for your dinner, and don't quarrel over it, for you will get nothing more."

Grethel took the bread under her charge, for Hansel'e pockets were full of pebbles. Then the stepmother led them a long way into the forest. They had gone but a very short distance when Hansel looked back at the house, and this he did again and again.

At last his stepmother said: "Why do you keep staying behind and looking back so?"

"Oh, mother," said the boy, "I can see my little white cat sitting on the roof of the house, and I am sure she is crying for me."

"Nonsense," she replied; "that is not your cat; it is the morning sun shining on the chimney pot."

Hansel had seen no cat, but he stayed behind every time to drop a white pebble from his pocket on the ground as they walked.

As soon as they reached a thick part of the wood their stepmother said:

"Come, children, gather some wood and I will make a fire, for it is very cold here."

Then Hansel and Grethel raised quite a high heap of brushwood and fagots, which soon blazed up into a bright fire, and the woman said to them:

"Sit down here, children, and rest, while I go and find your father, who is cutting wood in the forest; when we have finished our work we will come again and fetch you."

Hansel and Grethel seated themselves by the fire, and when noon arrived they each ate the piece of bread which their stepmother had given them for their dinner; and as long as they heard the strokes of the ax they felt safe, for they believed that their father was working near them. But it was not an ax they heard — only a branch which still hung on a withered tree, and was moved up and down by the wind. At last, when they had been sitting there a long time, the ohildren's eyes became heavy with fatigue and they fell fast asleep. When they awoke it was dark night, and poor Grethel began to cry, and said: "Oh, how shall we get out of the wood?"

But Hansel comforted her. "Don't fear," he said; "let us wait a little while till the moon rises, and then we shall easily find our way home."

Very soon the full moon rose, and then Hansel took his little sister by the hand, and the white pebble stones, which glittered like newly coined money in the moonlight, and which Hansel had dropped as he walked, pointed out the way. They walked all the night through, and did not reach their father's house till break of day.

They knocked at the door, and when their stepmother opened it, she exclaimed: "You naughty children, why have you been staying so long in the forest? We thought you were never coming back." But their father was overjoyed to see them, for it grieved him to the heart to think that they had been left alone in the woods.

Not long after this there came another time of scarcity and want in every house, and the children heard their stepmother talking after they were in bed. "The times are as bad as ever," she said; "we have just half a loaf left, and when that is gone all love will be at an end. The children must go away; we will take them deeper into the forest this time, and they will not be able to find their way home as they did before; it is the only plan to save ourselves from starvation." But the husband felt heavy at heart, for he thought it was better to share the last morsel with his children.

His wife would listen to nothing he said, but continued to reproach him, and as he had given way to her the first time, he could not refuse to do so now. The children were awake and heard all the conversation; so, as soon as their parents slept, Hansel got up, intending to go out and gather some more of the bright pebbles to let fall as he walked, that they might point out the way home; but his stepmother had locked the door and he could not open it. When he went back to his bed, he told his little sister not to fret, but to go to sleep in peace, for he was sure they would be taken care of.

Early the next morning the stepmother came and pulled the children out of bed, and when they were dressed, gave them each a piece of bread for their dinners, smaller than they had had before, and then they started on their way to the wood.

As they walked Hansel, who had the bread in his pocket, broke off little crumbs, and stopped every now and then to drop one, turning round as if he was looking back at his home.

"Hansel," said the woman, "what are you stopping for in that way? Come along directly!"

"I saw my pigeon sitting on the roof, and he wants to say good-by to me," replied the boy.

"Nonsense," she said; "that is not your pigeon; it is only the morning sun shining on the chimney-pot."

But Hansel did not look back any more; he only dropped pieces of bread behind him as they walked through the wood. This time they went on till they reached the thickest and densest part of the forest, where they had never been before in all their lives. Again they gathered fagots and brushwood, of which the stepmother made up a large fire. Then she said, "Remain here, children, and rest, while I go to help your father, who is cutting wood in the forest; when you feel tired, you can lie down and sleep for a little while, and we will come and fetch you in the evening when your father has finished his work."

So the children remained alone till midday, and then Grethel shared her piece of bread with Hansel, for he had scattered his own all along the road as they walked. After this they slept for a while, and the evening drew on; but no one came to fetch the poor children. When they awoke it was quite dark, and poor little Grethel was afraid; but Hansel comforted her as he had done before, by telling her they need only wait till the moon rose. "You know, little sister," he said, "that I have thrown bread crumbs all along the road we came, and they will easily point out the way home."

But when they went out of the thicket into the moonlight they found no bread crumbs, for the numerous birds which inhabited the trees of the forest had picked them all up. Hansel tried to hide his fear when he made this sad discovery, and said to his sister, "Cheer up, Grethel; I dare say we shall find our way home without the crumbs. Let us try." But this they found impossible. They wandered about the whole night, and the next day from morning till evening; but they could not get out of the wood, and were so hungry that had it not been for a few berries which they picked they must have starved.

At last they were so tired that their poor little legs could carry them no further; so they laid themselves down under a tree and went to sleep. When they awoke it was the third morning since they had left their father's house, and they determined to try once more to find their way home; but it was no use, they only went still deeper into the wood, and knew that if no help came they must starve.

About noon they saw a beautiful snow-white bird sitting on the branch of a tree, and singing so beautifully that they sood still to listen. When he had finished his song, he spread out his wings and flew on before them. The children followed him till at last they saw at a distance a small house; and the bird flew and perched on the roof.

But how surprised were the boy and girl, when they came nearer, to find that the house was built of gingerbread and ornamented with sweet cakes and tarts, while the window was formed of barley sugar. "Oh!" exclaimed Hansel, "let us stop here and have a splendid feast. I will have a piece from the roof first, Grethel; and you can eat some of the barley sugar window; it tastes so nice." Hansel reached up on tiptoe, and breaking off a piece of the gingerbread, he began to eat with all his might, for he was very hungry. Grethel seated herself on the doorstep, and began munching away at the cakes of which it was made. Presently a voice came out of the cottage:

"Munching, crunching, munching, Who's eating up my house!"

Then answered the children,

"The wind, the wind, only the wind!" and went on eating as if they never meant to leave off, without a suspicion of wrong. Hansel, who found the cake on the roof tasted very good, broke off another large piece, and Grethel had just taken out a whole pane of barley sugar from the window, and seated herself to eat it, when the door opened and a strange-looking old woman came out leaning on a stick.

Hansel and Grethel were so frightened that they let fall what they held in their hands. The old woman shook her head at them, and said: "Ah, you dear children, who has brought you here? Come in and stay with me for a little while, and there shall no harm happen to you." She seized them both by the hands as she spoke, and led them into the house. She gave them for supper plenty to eat and drink—milk and pancakes and sugar, apples and nuts; and when evening came, Hansel and Grethel were shown two beautiful little beds with white curtains, and they lay down in them and thought they were in heaven.

But though the old woman pretended to be friendly, she was a wicked witch who had her house built of gingerbread on purpose to entrap children. When once they were in her power, she would feed them well till they got fat and then kill them and cook them for her dinner; and this she called her feast day. Fortunately the witch had weak eyes and could not see very well; but she had a very keen scent, as wild animals have, and could easily discover when human beings were near. As Hansel and Grethel had approached her cottage, she laughed to herself maliciously, and said with a sneer: "I have them now; they shall not escape from me again!"

Early in the morning, before the children were awake, she was up, standing by their beds; and when she saw how beautiful they looked in their sleep, with their round, rosy cheeks, she muttered to herself: "What nice tidbits they will be!" Then she laid hold of Hansel with her rough hand, dragged him out of bed, and led him to a little cage which had a lattice door, and shut him in; he might scream as much as he would, but it was all useless.

After this she went back to Grethel, and shaking her roughly till she woke, cried: "Get up, you lazy hussy, and draw some water, that I may boil something good for your brother, who is shut up in a cage outside till he gets fat; and then I shall cook him and eat him!" When Grethel heard this she began to cry bitterly, but it was all useless; she was obliged to do as the wicked witch told her.

For poor Hansel's breakfast the best of everything was cooked; but Grethel had nothing for herself but a crab's claw. Every morning the old woman would go out to the little cage, and say: "Hansel, stick out your finger, that I may feel if you are fat enough for eating." But Hansel, who knew how dim her old eyes were, always stuck a bone through the bars of his cage, which she thought was his finger, for she could not see; and when she felt how thin it was, she wondered very much why he did not get fat.

However, as the weeks went on, and Hansel seemed not to get any fatter, she became impatient, and said she could not wait any longer. "Go, Grethel," she cried to the maiden, "be quick and draw water; Hansel may be fat or lean, I don't care; to-morrow morning I mean to kill him and cook him!"

Oh! how the poor little sister grieved when she was forced to draw the water; and as the tears rolled down her cheeks she exclaimed: "It would have been better to be eaten by wild beasts or to have been starved to death in the woods; then we should have died together!"

"Stop your crying!" cried the old woman; "it is not of the least use; no one will come to help you."

Early in the morning Grethel was obliged to go out and fill the great pot with water and hang it over the fire to boil. As soon as this was done the old woman said: "We will bake some bread first; I have made the oven hot and the dough is already kneaded." Then she dragged poor little Grethel up to the oven door, under which the flames were burning fiercely, and said: "Creep in there and see if it is hot enough yet to bake bread." But if Grethel had obeyed her she would have shut the poor child in and baked her for dinner, instead of boiling Hansel.

Grethel, however, guessed what she wanted to do, and said, "I don't know how to get in through that narrow door."

"Stupid goose," said the old woman, "why, the oven door is quite large enough for me; just look, I could get in myself." As she spoke she stepped forward and pretended to put her head in the oven.

A sudden thought gave Grethel unusual strength; she started forward, gave the old woman a push which sent her right into the oven, then she shut the iron door and fastened the bolt.

Oh, how the old witch did howl! It was quite horrible to hear her. But Grethel ran away, and therefore she was left to burn, just as she had left many poor little children to burn. And how quickly Grethel ran to Hansel, opened the door of his cage, and cried, "Hansel, Hansel, we are free! the old witch is dead!" He flew like a bird out of his cage at these words as soon as the door was opened and the children were so overjoyed that they ran into each other's arms, and kissed each other with the greatest love.

And now that there was nothing to be afraid of, they went back into the house, and while looking round the old witch's room they saw an old oak chest, which they opened, and found it full of pearls and precious stones.

"These are better than pebbles," said Hansel; and he filled his pockets as full as they would hold.

"I will carry some home, too," said Grethel, and she held out her apron, which held quite as much as Hansel's pockets.

"We will go now," he said, "and get away as soon as we can from this enchanted forest."

They had been walking for nearly two hours when they came to a large piece of water.

"What shall we do now?" said the boy. "We cannot get across, and there is no bridge of any sort."

"Oh, here comes a boat!" cried Grethel, but she was mistaken; it was only a white duck which came swimming toward the children. "Perhaps she will help us across if we ask her," said the child; and she sang, "Little duck, do help poor Hansel and Grethel; there is not a bridge, nor a boat — will you let us sail across on your white back?"

The good-natured duck came near the bank as Grethel spoke, so close indeed that Hansel could seat himself, and wanted to take his little sister on his lap, but she said, "No, we shall be too heavy for the kind duck; let her take us over one at a time."

The good creature did as the children wished; she carried Grethel over first, and then came back for Hansel. And then how happy the children were to find themselves in a part of the wood which they remembered quite well, and as they walked on the more familiar it became, till at last they caught sight of their father's house. Then they began to run, and, bursting into the room, threw themselves into their father's arms.

Poor man, he had not had a moment's peace since the children had been left alone in the forest; he was full of joy at finding them safe and well again, and now they had nothing to fear, for their wicked stepmother was dead.

But how surprised the poor woodcutter was when Grethel opened and shook her little apron to see the glittering pearls and precious stones scattered about the room, while Hansel drew handful after handful from his pockets. From this moment all his care and sorrow were at an end, and the father lived in happiness with his children till his death.

The Widow's Two Daughters
Jakob and Wilhelm Grimm

A Widow, who lived in a cottage at some little distance from the village, had two daughters, one of whom was beautiful and industrious, the other idle and ugly. But this ugly one the mother loved best, because she was her own child; and she cared so little for the other that she made her do all the work, and be quite a Cinderella in the house.

Poor maiden, she was obliged to go every day and seat herself by the side of a well which stood in the broad high-road, and here she had to sit and spin till her fingers bled.

One day when the spindle was so covered with blood that she could not use it, she rose and dipped it in the water of the well to wash it. While she was doing so it slipped from her hand and fell to the bottom. In terror and tears, she ran and told her stepmother what had happened.

The woman scolded her in a most violent manner, and was so merciless that she said: "As you have let the spindle fall into the water, you may go in and fetch it out, for I will not buy another."

Then the maiden went back to the well and, hardly knowing what she was about in her distress of mind, threw herself into the water to fetch the spindle.

At first she lost all consciousness, but presently, as her senses returned, she found herself in a beautiful meadow, on which the sun was brightly shining and thousands of flowers grew.

She walked a long way across this meadow, till she came to a baker's oven which was full of new bread, and the loaves cried, "'Ah, pull us out! pull us out! or we shall burn, we have been so long baking!"

Then she stepped near to the oven and with the breadshovel took the loaves all out.

She walked on after this, and presently came to a tree full of apples, and the tree cried, "Shake me! shake me! my apples are all quite ripe!"

Then she shook the tree till the fruit fell around her like rain, and at last there was not one more left upon it. After this she gathered the apples into one large heap, and went on further.

At last she came to a small house, and looking earnestly at it she saw an old woman peeping out, who had such large teeth that the girl was quite frightened, and turned to run away.

But the old woman cried after her: "What dost thou fear, dear child? Come and live here with me, and do all the work in the house, and I will make you so happy. You must, however, take care to make my bed well, and to shake it with energy, for then the feathers fly about, and in the world they will say it snows, for I am Mother Holle." As the old woman talked in this kind manner, she won the maiden's heart, so that she readily agreed to enter her service.

She was very anxious to keep friendly with her, and took care to shake up the bed well, so that the feathers might fly down like snowflakes. Therefore she had a very happy life with Mother Holle. She had plenty to eat and drink, and never heard an angry word.

But after she had stayed a long time with the kind old woman, she began to feel sad, and could not explain to herself why, till at last she discovered that she was homesick. And it seemed to her a thousand times better to go home than to stay with Mother Holle, although she made her so happy.

And the longing to go home grew so strong that at last she was obliged to speak.

"Dear Mother Holle," she said, "you have been very kind to me, but I have such sorrow in my heart that I cannot stay here any longer; I must return to my own people."

"Then," said Mother Holle, "I am pleased to hear that you are longing to go home, and as you have served me so well and truly, I will show you the way myself."

So she took her by the hand and led her to a broad gateway. The gate was open, and as the young girl passed through there fell upon her a shower of gold, which clung to her dress and remained hanging to it, so that she was bedecked with gold from head to foot.

"That is your reward for having been so industrious," and as the old woman spoke she placed in her hand the spindle which had fallen into the well.

Then the great gate was closed and the maiden found herself once more in the world, and not far from her stepmother's house. As she entered the farm-yard a cock perched on the wall crowed loudly, and cried: "Kikerika! our golden lady is come home, I see!"

Then she went in to her stepmother; and because she was so bedecked with gold both the mother and sister welcomed her kindly. The maiden related all that had happened to her; and when the mother heard how much Wealth had been gained by her stepdaughter, she was anxious that her own ugly and idle daughter should try her fortune in the same way.

So she made her go and sit on the well and spin; and the girl, who wanted all the riches without working for them, did not spin fast enough to make her fingers bleed.

So she pricked her finger, and pushed her hand in the thorn bushes, till at last a few spots of blood dropped on the spindle.

Directly she saw these spots she let it drop into the water and sprang in after it herself. Just as her sister had done, she found herself in a beautiful meadow, and walked for some distance along the same path till she came to the baker's oven.

She heard the loaves cry, "Pull us out! pull us out! or we shall burn; we have been here so long baking!"

But the idle girl answered, "No, indeed; I have no wish to soil my hands with your dirty oven;" and so she walked on till she came to the apple-tree.

"Shake me! shake me!" it cried; "for my apples are quite ripe!"

"I don't agree to that at all," she replied, "for some of the apples might fall on my head," and as she spoke she walked lazily on further.

Then she at last stood before the door of Mother Holle's house she had no fear of her great teeth, for she had heard all about them from her sister; so she walked right up to her and offered to be her servant. Mother Holle accepted the offer of her services, and for a whole day the young girl was very industrious and did everything that was told her; for she thought of the gold that was to be poured upon her.

But on the second day she gave way to her laziness, and on the third it was worse. Several days passed, and she would not get up in the mornings at the proper hour. The bed was never made or shaken, so that feathers could fly about, till at last Mother Holle was quite tired of her, and said she must go away; that her services were not wanted any more.

The lazy girl was quite overjoyed at going, and thought the golden rain was sure to come when Mother Holle led her to the gate. But as she passed under it a large kettle full of pitch was upset over her.

"That is the reward for your Service," said the old woman as she shut the gate.

So the idle girl walked home with the pitch sticking all over her, and as she entered the court the cock on the wall cried out:

"Kikeriki! our smutty young lady is come home, I see!"

The pitch stuck closely, and hung all about her hair and her clothes, and do what she would as long as she lived it never would come off.

Little Red Riding-Hood

Charles Perrault

Once upon a time there was a little girl who was called Little Red Riding-Hood, because she was quite small and because she always wore a red cloak with a big red hood to it, which her grandmother had made for her.

Now one day her mother, who had been churning and baking cakes, said to her:

"My dear, put on your red cloak with the hood to it, and take this cake and this pot of butter to your Grannie, and ask how she is, for I hear she is ailing."

Now Little Red Riding-Hood was very fond of her grandmother, who made her so many nice things, so she put on her cloak joyfully and started on her errand. But her grandmother lived some way off, and to reach the cottage Little Red Riding-Hood had to pass through a vast lonely forest. However, some wood-cutters were at work in it, so Little Red Riding-Hood was not so very much alarmed when she saw a great big wolf coming towards her, because she knew that wolves were cowardly things.

And sure enough the wolf, though but for the wood cutters would surely have eaten Little Red Riding-Hood, only stopped and asked her politely where she was going.

"I am going to see Grannie, take her this cake and this pot of butter, and ask how she is," says Little Red Riding-Hood.

"Does she live a very long way off? " asks the wolf craftily.

"Not so very far if you go by the straight road," replied Little Red Riding-Hood. "You only have to pass the mill and the first cottage on the right is Grannie's; but I am going by the wood path because there are such a lot of nuts and flowers and butterflies."

"I wish you good luck," says the wolf politely. "Give my respects to your grandmother and tell her I hope she is quite well."

And with that he trotted off. But instead of going his ways he turned back, took the straight road to the old woman's cottage, and knocked at the door.

Rap! Rap! Rap!

"Who's there?" asked the old woman, who was in bed.

"Little Red Riding-Hood," sings out the wolf, making his voice as shrill as he could. "I've come to bring dear Grannie a pot of butter and a cake from mother, and to ask how you are."

"Pull the bobbin, and the latch will go up," says the old woman, well satisfied.

So the wolf pulled the bobbin, the latch went up, and — oh my! — it wasn't a minute before he had gobbled up old Grannie, for he had had nothing to eat for a week.

Then he shut the door, put on Grannie's night-cap, and, getting into bed, rolled himself well up in the clothes.

By and by along comes little Red Riding-Hood, who had been amusing herself by gathering nuts, running after butterflies, and picking flowers.

So she knocked at the door.

Rap! Rap! Rap!

"Who's there?" says the wolf, making his voice as soft as he could.

Now Little Red Riding-Hood heard the voice was very gruff, but she thought her grandmother had a cold; so she said:

"Little Red Riding-Hood, with a pot of butter and a cake from mother, to ask how you are."

"Pull the bobbin, and the latch will go up."

So Little Red Riding-Hood pulled the bobbin, the latch went up, and there, she thought, was her grandmother in the bed; for the cottage was so dark one could not see well. Besides, the crafty wolf turned his face to the wall at first. And he made his voice as soft, as soft as he could, when he said:

"Come and kiss me, my dear."

Then Little Red Riding-Hood took off her cloak and went to the bed.

"Oh, Grandmamma, Grandmamma," says she, "what big arms you've got!"

"All the better to hug you with," says he.

"But, Grandmamma, Grandmamma, what big legs you've got!"

"All the better to run with, my dear."

"Oh, Grandmamma, Grandmamma, what big ears you've got!"

"All the better to hear with, my dear."

"But, Grandmamma, Grandmamma, what big eyes you've got!"

"All the better to see you with, my dear!"

"Oh, Grandmamma, Grandmamma, what big teeth you've got!"

"All the better to eat you with, my dear!" says that wicked, wicked wolf, and with that he gobbled up little Red Riding-Hood.

Puss in Boots
Charles Perrault

Once, a poor miller had only his mill, his ass and his cat to divide among his three sons when he died. The children shared out their patrimony and did not bother to call in any lawyers. Had they done so, they would have lost everything. Therefore, the eldest took the mill, the second the ass, and the youngest was left with only the cat.

He felt himself very ill used, and said to himself:

"My brothers can earn an honest living with their inheritance, but once I've eaten my cat and made a collar with his fur, I shall die of hunger."

The cat, overhearing him, decided to pretend he had not heard. He addressed his master gravely.

"Master, give me a bag and a pair of boots to protect my little feet from the brambles and you'll see that your father has provided for you quite well, after all."

Although the master could not really believe his cat would support him, he had seen him play such cunning tricks when he caught rats and mice (he would hang upside down by his feet; or hide himself in the meal, or play at being dead) that he had some hope his cat might have a helpful scheme.

When the cat had what he asked for, he put on his fine boots and slung the bag round his neck, keeping hold of the draw-strings with his two front paws. He went to a warren where he knew there were a great many rabbits. He put some grain and a selection of cloves at the bottom of the bag and then laid quite still, like a corpse, waiting for some foolish young rabbit to come and investigate the bag and its contents.

No sooner had he waited when a rabbit jumped into the bag. Instantly, the cat pulled the draw-strings tight and killed him.

Bearing his prey, he went to the King and asked to speak to him. Everyone was impressed at court by the cat's bearing, so he was led to the King's private apartment. As soon as he got inside the door, he bowed elegantly and said:

"Majesty, I present you with a young rabbit that my master, the Marquis of Carabas (the cat had decided to call him that), commanded me to offer you, with his humblest compliments."

"Tell your master that I thank him with all my heart," said the King.

Another day, the cat hid himself in the corn, holding his bag open. Two partridges flew into it, so he pulled the strings tight. Then he again went to the King, just as before. The King accepted the partridges with delight and rewarded the cat with a handsome tip.

The cat continued to take his master's game to the King for two or three months. One day, he discovered that the King was to take a drive along the riverside with his daughter, the most beautiful princess in any land. The cat said to his master:

"Take my advice and your fortune is made. Go and swim in the river at a spot I will show to you and I will look after the rest."

The Marquis of Carabas obeyed his cat, although he could not think why he should do so. While he was bathing, the King drove by and the cat cried out forcefully:

"Help! Help! The Marquis of Carabas is drowning!"

The King put his head out of his carriage window when he heard this commotion and recognised the cat. He ordered his servants to go and save the Marquis of Carabas.

While they were pulling the marquis out of the river, the cat went to the King's carriage and told him how robbers had stolen his master's clothes while he swam in the river. (Actually, the cunning cat had hidden the miller's son's wretched clothes under a stone.)

The King ordered his wardrobe master to return to the palace and bring some of his own finest garments for the Marquis to wear. When the young man put them on, the King's daughter thought that he was a very handsome young man. When the Marquis of Carabas showed her such respect and tenderness that she fell completely in love with him.

The King invited the Marquis of Carabas to join him in his carriage and continue the drive in style. The cat was quite proud to see that his scheme was a success and marched ahead of the procession, coming to some peasants who were mowing a meadow, he announced:

"Good people, tell the King that this meadow belongs to the Marquis of Carabas, or I'll see that you are chopped into very small pieces!"

When he saw the mowers, the King asked them who owned the hay-field. They had been so frightened by the cat that they all said:

"It belongs to the Marquis of Carabas."

The King told the marquis that his estate looked very rich indeed.

The cat again raced ahead of the procession and seeing some harvesters, said:

"Good harvesters, tell the King these cornfields belong to the Marquis of Carabas, or I'll chop you into very small pieces!"

When the King passed by a little later, he asked of the harvesters:

"Who owns this field of corn?"

"The Marquis of Carabas," they answered, fearing the cat.

The King even more began to admire the Marquis. The cat ran before the carriage and made the same threats to everyone he met on the way; the King was perfectly astonished at the young man's great possessions.

Then, the cat arrived at a castle. In this castle lived an ogre, who was extraordinarily rich for he was the true owner of all the land through which the King had travelled. The cat had taken the time to find out about this ogre and now he asked the servant who answered the door if he could speak to him. "I cannot pass so close by this castle without paying my respects to its owner."

The ogre made him welcome in his castle.

The cat, always clever, said:

"I'm told you can transform yourself into all sorts of animals, and that you can change yourself into a lion, or even an elephant."

"Quite right," replied the ogre. "Just to show you, I'll turn myself into a lion."

When he found himself face to face with the lion, even our cat was so scared that he jumped up on to the roof and knelt there shaking in fear because his boots weren't made for walking on tiles.

When the ogre became himself again, the cat jumped down and confessed how terrified he had been.

"But I hear—though I can scarcely believe it—that you also have the power to take the shapes of the very smallest animals. Can you truly shrink down as small as a rat, or a mouse? I must admit, even if it seems rude, that I think that's quite impossible."

"Impossible?" said the ogre. "Just you see!" and he changed into a mouse and began to scamper around the room. The cat immediately jumped on him and gobbled him up.

Meanwhile, the King saw the ogre's fine castle as he drove by and decided to pay it a visit. The cat hearing the sound of the carriage wheels on the drawbridge, ran outside and greeted the king.

"Welcome, your majesty, to the castle of the Marquis of Carabas."

"What sir? Does this fine castle also belong to you? I've never seen anything more wonderful than this courtyard and the walls that surround it. May we be permitted to view the interior?" The marquis gave his hand to the young princess and followed the King. They entered a grand room where they found a banquet ready prepared; the ogre had invited all his friends to a dinner party, but none of the guests dared enter the castle when they saw the King had arrived. The King was delighted with the riches of the Marquis of Carabas, and his daughter was beside herself about him. After his fifth or sixth glass of wine, the King said:

"Simply ask, my fine fellow, and you shall have my daughter's hand."

The Marquis bowed very low, immediately accepted the honour the King bestowed on him and married the princess that very day. The cat was made a great lord and never again chased mice, except as a diversion.

Rapunzel

Jakob and Wilhelm Grimm

There was once a man who lived all alone with his wife in a little house, the back windows of which looked upon a magnificent garden. But around this garden was a high wall, and no one ever ventured into it, because it belonged to an old witch, who had great magic powers, so that every one was afraid of her.

One day the wife was standing at her window, looking down at this garden, when it chanced that she saw a bed of radishes which looked so green and fresh that she immediately had a great longing to eat some of them. Day by day the longing grew, but as, of course, she could not have the radishes, she became pale and worn with thinking of them.

Her husband was sorry to see her look like this, and asked, "What ails you, dear wife?"

Then she told him how much she wished for some of the radishes growing in the next garden, and as he loved her very dearly he made up his mind that, no matter what it cost him, she should have her wish. So in the evening when it was dusk, he slipped over the wall into the witch's garden, grasped a handful of radishes, and brought them to his wife.

She made a salad of them and ate them with relish, but they were so good that the next day she longed for more, and her husband felt that he would have no rest until she had her desire.

So he waited until the evening came, and then once more slipped down over the garden wall, but oh! how frightened he was when he found himself face to face with the old witch.

"How dare you come into my garden like a thief and steal my radishes?" she cried, with angry looks. "See if I do not make you suffer for your rashness."

"Forgive me," cried the poor man, "for I have only erred from necessity. My wife, who had seen the radishes from our window, would have died of longing if she had not had some."

The witch appeared to be softened, and told him that he might take as many radishes as he pleased. "But," said she, "in return you must promise me your first little child. I will be good and kind to it and it shall want for nothing."

The man was so frightened that he said, "Yes," and then the witch allowed him to go.

Now, it happened that the man and his wife had no children, but soon afterward a little baby girl came to them, and at once the witch appeared, gave the child the name of Rapunzel (which means a sort of radish), and carried it away with her.

Rapunzel was the most beautiful child under the sun. When she was twelve years old the witch shut her up in a tower which had neither staircase nor door, only a small window, right at the very top of it.

When the old witch wanted to come in, she stood below and cried, "Rapunzel, let down your hair!"

Rapunzel had magnificent long hair, as fine as spun gold, and when she heard the witch's voice, she unbounded her long plaits, wound them round the hasp of the window and then let fall twenty ells of hair, and up this hair the old witch climbed.

After a year or two it chanced that the King's son was riding through the wood, and came to the tower. There he heard such beautiful singing that he was forced to stand and listen.

It was Rapunzel, singing to while away the time. The King's son at once wished to go to her, and sought in vain for either a door or a staircase.

He rode slowly homeward, but the song had touched his heart so that he could not help but return, day by day, to listen to the music.

One day, as he stood behind a tree, he saw the witch arrive, and heard her call: "Rapunzel, Rapunzel, let down your hair!"

And Rapunzel let down her locks of hair, up which the old woman climbed.

"Ah!" said the Prince, "if that is the ladder one has to climb, I will try my luck. "

The next day, when it began to get dark, he went to the tower, and cried, "Rapunzel, Rapunzel, let down your hair." At once the hair came tumbling down, and the King's son mounted.

Oh! how frightened Rapunzel was when she saw a man jump in through the window, for she had never seen one before. But the Prince was very kind and friendly, and told her how his heart had been so touched by her sweet singing that he had known no rest until he had seen the singer.

So Rapunzel ceased to be afraid, and when he asked her if she would like him for a husband, she laid her hand in his, and said, "Yes." For she thought, "He is young and handsome, and he will love me better than old Dame Gothel." But then she said, "Although I would willingly go with you, I do not know how I am to get down. Whenever you come to see me, you must bring a skein of silk with you, and I will weave it into a ladder; then, when it is ready I can climb down it, and you can carry me away upon your horse."

Then they agreed that the Prince should only visit her in the evening, because the old witch always came in the daytime. All went well until one day Rapunzel said to the witch:

"I wonder how it is, Dame Gothel, that you are so much heavier for me to draw up than the King's son — he is with me in a moment."

"You wicked child!" cried the witch. "What is this I hear? I thought I had separated you from all the world, and yet you have deceived me."

In her anger, she clutched Rapunzel's beautiful hair, and, seizing a pair of scissors, snip, snap! she cut it all off, and the thick plaits lay upon the ground.

And so merciless was she that she carried poor Rapunzel away to a desert place, where she was forced to live in great grief and misery.

On the very same day, she made Rapunzel's golden locks fast to the window hasp, and when the King's son came in the evening, and cried, "Rapunzel, Rapunzel, let down your hair," she let it down.

The Prince mounted, but alas! instead of his dear Rapunzel, he found the old witch, who gazed at him with angry, venomous eyes.

"Aha!" she cried mockingly. "So you came to fetch your dear little wife, eh? But the singing-bird is no longer in its nest; the cat has carried it away and will scratch out your eyes for you too. Rapunzel is lost to you forever — you will never see her again."

The Prince was beside himself with grief, and in his despair he leaped from the tower, and although he did not lose his life, the thorns into which he fell pierced his eyes and blinded him.

So he roamed blindly through the woods, living upon roots and berries, and doing nothing but grieve over the loss of his dear wife.

For many years he wandered about in misery, and came at length to the desert place in which Rapunzel was living.

He heard a sweet voice, which seemed so familiar to him that he went toward it and as soon as Rapunzel saw him, she recognized him and fell upon his neck and wept. Then two of her tears ran down and moistened his eyes, and at once they were healed, and he could see as clearly as before.

The Prince led Rapunzel home to his kingdom, where they were received with great joy, and where they lived in happiness and contentment for many, many years.

Cinderella
Jakob and Wilhelm Grimm

Once upon a time the wife of a rich man fell sick, and as she knew her end was approaching, she called her only daughter to her bedside, and said: "Dear child, when I am gone continue good and pious, and Heaven will help you in every trouble, and I will be your guardian angel."

Soon after this the mother closed her eyes in death, and day after day the maiden went to her mother's grave to weep. But she never forgot her last words, and continued pious and gentle to all around her. Winter came and covered the grave with its dazzling drapery of snow; but when the bright sun of spring again warmed the earth the husband had taken to himself another wife. This wife had been already married, and she brought with her two daughters, who were fair and beautiful in appearance, while at heart they were evil-minded and malicious. It soon became a very sad time for their poor step-sister, of whom they were very envious, and at last persuaded their mother to send her to the kitchen.

"Is the stupid goose to sit in the parlor with us?" they said. "Those who eat ought to work. Send her into the kitchen with the kitchen-maid."

Then they took away all her nice clothes and gave her an ugly old frock and wooden shoes, which she was obliged to put on.

"Look at our fine princess now! See how she has dressed herself!" they said, laughing and driving her into the kitchen.

And there she was obliged to remain doing hard work from morning till night, and she had to rise early to draw water, to light the fire, to cook, and to wash. Besides all this, her stepsisters invented all sorts of ways to make her more unhappy. They would either treat her with scorn or else push her out of their way so roughly that she sometimes fell among the pea shells and cabbage leaves that lay in the yard.

At night, when she was tired with her work, she had no bed to lie on, and when the weather was cold she would creep into the ashes on the warm hearth, and get so black and smutty that they gave her the name of Cinderella.

It happened one day that the father was going to a fair, and he asked his two stepdaughters what he should bring back for them as a present.

"A beautiful dress," said the eldest; "a pearl necklace," said her sister. "And, Cinderella," asked her father, "what will you have?"

"Father," she replied, "please bring me the first twig that strikes your hat on your way home."

So the father bought for his stepdaughters a beautiful dress and a pearl necklace, and as he was returning home, he rode through a shrubbery where the green bushes clustered thickly around him, and a hazel twig, stretching across his path struck his hat. Then he stopped, broke off the twig, and carried it home with him.

As soon as he reached the house he gave his stepdaughters the presents they had wished for, and to Cinderella the hazel twig from the hazel bush. She thanked him for it even more than her sisters had done for their beautiful presents, and went out immediately to her mother's grave, where she planted the hazel twig, and wept over it so much that her tears fell and softened the earth.

The twig grew and became a beautiful tree, and Cinderella went three times every day to pray and weep at the grave; and on each visit a little white bird would perch on the tree, and when she expressed a wish, the bird would throw down whatever she wished for.

After a time the king of the country gave a grand ball, which was to continue for three days. All the beautiful young ladies in the land were invited to this ball, that the king's son might make choice of a bride from among them.

The two stepsisters, when they heard that they were invited, knew not how to contain themselves for joy. They called Cinderella in haste, and said: "Come and dress our hair and trim our shoes with gold buckles, for we are going to the ball at the king's palace."

When Cinderella heard this she began to cry, for she was fond of dancing, and she wanted to go with her stepsisters, so she went to her stepmother and begged to be allowed to accompany them.

"You, Cinderella!" cried her stepmother, "so covered with dirt and smut as you are; you go to a bath. Besides, you have no dress nor dancing shoes."

Cinderella, however, continued to beg for permission to go, till her stepmother said at last:

"There, go away into the kitchen; I have just thrown a shovelful of linseed into the ashes; if you can pick these seeds all out and bring them to me in two hours, you shall go."

Away went the maiden through the back door into the garden, and called out:

"Little tame pigeons,
    Turtle-doves too,
If you don't help me,
    What shall I do?

> Come, pick up the seeds,
>   All the birds in the sky,
> For I cannot do it
>   In time if I try."

Then came flying in at the kitchen window two pretty white doves, and they were followed by all the birds of the air, twittering in a swarm. Nodding their heads at Cinderella, they began to pick, pick, and very quickly picked every seed from the ashes, till the shovel was full. It was all finished in one hour, and then the birds spread their wings and flew away.

Full of joy, the maiden carried the shovelful of seed to her stepmother, believing that now she was sure to go to the ball. But her stepmother said:

"No, Cinderella, you have no dress, and you have not learned to dance; you would only be laughed at."

Still she cried and begged so hard to be allowed to go that her stepmother, to keep her quiet, threw two shovelfuls of linseed in the ashes this time, and told her she should go if she picked all these out in two hours.

"She can never do that in the time," thought the cruel woman as Cinderella ran away to the kitchen; but the maiden went again into the garden and called the birds:

> "Little tame pigeons,
>   Turtle doves, too,
> If you don't help me,
>   What shall I do?
> Come, pick up the seeds,
>   All the birds in the sky,
> For I cannot do it
>   In time if I try."

Then the birds all came as before, and in less than an hour every seed was picked out and laid in the shovels. As soon as they had flown away Cinderella carried the shovelfuls of seed to her stepmother, quite expecting now to go to the ball with her stepsisters. But she said again:

"It is of no use to fret, Cinderella; you have no dress, you cannot dance, and were you to go it would be a disgrace to us all."

Then she turned her back on the poor girl and hastened away with her two proud daughters to the ball. There was no one at home now but Cinderella, so she went out to her mother's grave and stood under the hazel tree and cried:

"Shake and shiver, little tree,
With gold and silver cover me!"

Then the bird in the tree threw down a beautiful silk dress embroidered with gold and silver, and a new pair of glittering golden slippers. In great haste she dressed herself in these beautiful clothes and went to the ball. When she entered the ball-room, looking so beautiful in her rich dress and slippers, her stepmother and sisters did not know her; indeed, they took her for a foreign princess. The idea that it could be Cinderella never entered their heads; they supposed she was safe at home picking linseed from the ashes.

The king's son took a great deal of notice of this unknown lady, and danced with her several times, till at last he would dance with no other, always saying: "This is my partner." So she danced all the evening till it was time to go home, and the prince said he would accompany her, for he wanted to discover were she lived. But she avoided him, and with one bound sprang into the pigeon house. The prince was quite astonished, but waited till nearly all the company had left, and then told his father that the strange lady was in the pigeon house.

"Could it be Cinderella?" thought the stepmother, who would not leave till the last; "I must find out." So she advised the prince to send for workmen to pull down the pigeon house. This was soon done, but they found no one there. When the stepmother and her daughters reached home, they found Cinderella in her smutty dress, lying in the ashes, and a dingy little lamp burning on the chimney-piece. The truth was, Cinderella had slipped out from the back of the pigeon house even more quickly than she had jumped in, and had run to the hazel tree. There she hastened to take off her beautiful clothes and lay them on the grave while she put on her kitchen clothes, and the bird came down and carried the ball dress away while Cinderella went home to lie in the ashes.

A short time after this the king gave another ball, to which her parents and stepsisters were invited. As soon as they were gone Cinderella went to the hazel tree and said:

"Shake and shiver, little tree,
Throw gold and silver over me!"

Then the bird threw down a far more elegant dress than the first, and when she entered the ballroom in her rich apparel, every one was astonished at her great beauty. The king's son, who refused to dance till she came, took her hand and led her to her seat, and during the whole evening he would dance with no one else, always saying: "This is my partner."

Again, when it was time to go, the prince wanted to accompany her and find out her home, but she managed to avoid him and rushed out into the garden behind the palace, in which grew a beautiful tree loaded with pears. She climbed like a squirrel between the branches, and the prince could not find her anywhere. When his father came home they even ordered the tree to be cut down, but no one could be found among the branches. The stepmother still had a fear that it might he Cinderella, but when they returned home there she was in her kitchen dress, lying among the ashes as usual. When they were looking for her she had sprung down at the other side of the tree, and the bird in the hazel tree had brought her kitchen clothes and taken away the ball dress.

A third fête took place, to which the stepmother and her daughters were invited, and Cinderella again went to her mother's grave and said to the tree:

"Shake and rustle, little tree,
Throw gold and silver over me!"

Then the bird threw down a most magnificent dress, more glittering and elegant than ever, and the brightest pair of gilded slippers.

When she appeared at the fête in this dress, every one was astonished at her beauty. The prince danced only with her, and to every other proposal replied: "This is my partner." When the time came to leave, Cinderella wanted to go, and the prince wished to accompany her, but she darted away from him and vanished so quickly that he could not follow her.

Now, the king's son had had recourse to stratagem in the hope of discovering the home of the lovely princess. He had ordered the steps of the castle to be strewn with pitch, so that as Cinderella hurried away her left slipper stuck to the steps, and she was obliged to leave it behind. The prince himself picked it up; it was very small and elegant, and covered with gold.

The next morning he sent for one of his servants and said to him, "None other shall be my bride but the lady to whom that slipper belongs, and whose foot it shall fit."

When the stepsisters heard of this proclamation from the prince they were delighted, for they both had small feet. The messenger went with the slipper from house to house, and the young ladies who had been present at the ball tried to put it on, but it would fit none of them, and at last he came to the two sisters. The eldest tried it on first in another room, and her mother stood by. She could have worn it if her great toe had not been so large, so her mother offered her a knife, and told her to cut it off. "When you are a queen," she said, "you will not want to use your feet much."

The maiden cut the toe off and forced on the slipper in spite of the pain, and the messenger led her to the prince. But on their road they had to pass the grave of Cinderella's mother, and on the hazel tree sat two doves, who cried:

"That is not the right bride,
  The slipper is much too small;
 Blood is flowing inside,
  The shoe does not fit her at all!"

Then the messenger examined the slipper and found it full of blood. So he led her back and told the next sister to try. She also went into another room with her mother, and found that she could not get the slipper over her heel.

"Cut a piece off," said her mother, offering her a knife; "when you are queen you will not have to use your feet much."

The maiden cut a piece off her heel, and fitted on the slipper in spite of the pain, and then went to the prince. They also had to pass the grave of Cinderella's mother, over which the two doves still sat and cried:

"Go back, go back,
  There is blood in the shoe;
 The shoe is too small —
  That bride will not do!"

So the messenger examined the shoe and found the white stocking quite red with blood. He took the false bride back to the house, and this time the king's son went with him.

"Hast thou not another daughter?" asked the prince of Cinderella's father.

"None," he said, "excepting the child of my first wife, a little Cinderella; she could not possibly be your bride."

"Send for her," said the prince.

But the stepmother answered: "Oh, no! I dare not let you see her — she is much too dirty."

But the prince insisted that Cinderella should be sent for, so at last they called her in.

After washing her hands and face, she made her appearance, and bowed to the prince, who offered her the golden shoe. She seated herself on a footstool, took off the heavy wooden shoe from her left foot, and slipped on the golden slipper, which fitted her exactly. Then, as she lifted up her head and looked at the prince, he recognized the beautiful maiden who had danced with him at the ball, and exclaimed: "That is the right bride!"

The stepmother and her two daughters were in a dreadful rage when they heard this, and turned white with anger.

But the prince disregarded their anger, and taking Cinderella on his horse rode away with her. As they passed the hazel tree on the grass, the two white doves cried:

> "Fair maid and true,
>> No blood in her shoe;
> She is the bride,
>> With the prince by her side!"

As they rode by the doves came and perched on Cinderella's shoulders, one on the right and the other on the left.

When the marriage day came the two stepsisters, wishing to share Cinderella's fortune, contrived to be present. As the bridal party walked to church, they placed themseives one on the right and the other on the left of the bride. On the way the doves picked out one eye from each of them. When returning they changed places, and the doves picked out the other eye of each, so they were for their wickedness and falsehood both punished with blindness during the rest of their lives.

Little Snow White
Jakob and Wilhelm Grimm

Long, long ago, in the winter-time, when the snowflakes were falling like little white feathers from the sky, a Queen sat beside her window, which was framed in black ebony, and stitched. As she worked, she looked sometimes at the falling snow, and so it happened that she pricked her finger with her needle, so that three drops of blood fell upon the snow. How pretty the red blood looked upon the dazzling white! The Queen said to herself as she saw it, "Ah me! if only I had a dear little child as white as the snow, as rosy as the blood, and with hair as black as the ebony window-frame."

Soon afterward a little daughter came to her, who was white as snow, rosy as the blood, and whose hair was as black as ebony—so she was called "Little Snow White." But alas! when the little one came, the good Queen died.

A year passed away, and the King took another wife. She was very beautiful, but so proud and haughty that she could not bear to be surpassed in beauty by any one. She possessed a wonderful mirror which could answer her when she stood before it and said:

"Mirror, mirror upon the wall,
Who is the fairest fair of all?"

The mirror answered:

"Thou, O Queen, art fairest of all."

and the Queen was contented, because she knew the mirror could speak nothing but the truth.

But as time passed on, Little Snow-White grew more and more beautiful until, when she was seven years old, she was as lovely as the bright day, and still more lovely than the Queen herself, so that when the lady one day asked her mirror:

"Mirror, mirror upon the wall,
Who is the fairest fair of all?"

"O Lady Queen, though fair ye be;
Snow-White is fairer far to see."

The Queen was horrified, and from that moment envy and pride grew in her heart like rank weeds, until one day she called a huntsman and said, "Take the child away into the woods and kill her, for I can no longer bear the sight of her. And when you return bring with you her heart, that I may know you have obeyed my will." The huntsman dared not disobey, so he led Snow White out into the woods and placed an arrow in his bow to pierce her innocent heart, but the little maid begged him to spare her life, and the child's beauty touched his heart with pity, so that he bade her run away. Then as a young wild boar came rushing by he killed it, took out its heart, and carried it home to the Queen.

Poor little Snow-White was now all alone in the wild wood, and so frightened was she that she trembled at every leaf that rustled. So she began to run, and ran on and on until she came to a little house, where she went in to rest.

In the little house everything she saw was tiny, but more dainty and clean than words can tell.

Upon a white-covered table stood seven little plates and upon each plate lay a little spoon, besides which there were seven knives and forks and seven little goblets. Against the wall, and side by side, stood seven little beds with snow-white sheets.

Snow-White was so hungry and thirsty that she took a little food from each of the seven plates, and drank a few drops of wine from each goblet, for she did not wish to take everything away from one. Then, because she was so tired, she crept into one bed after the other, seeking for rest; but one was too long, another too short, and so on, until she came to the seventh, which suited her exactly; so she said her prayers and soon fell fast asleep.

When night fell, the masters of the little house came home. They were seven dwarfs, who worked with a pick-axe and spade, searching for copper and gold in the heart of the mountains.

They lit their seven candles and then saw that some one had been to visit them. The first said, "Who has been sitting on my chair?"

The second said, "Who has been eating from my plate?"

The third, "Who has taken a piece of my bread?"

The fourth, "Who has taken some of my vegetables?"

The fifth, "Who has been using my fork?"

The sixth, "Who has been cutting with my knife?"

The seventh, "Who has been drinking out of my goblet?"

The first looked round and saw that his bed was rumpled, so he said, "Who has been getting into my bed?" Then the others looked round and each one cried, "Some one has been on my bed, too."

But the seventh saw little Snow-White lying asleep in his bed, and called the others to come and look at her; and they cried aloud with surprise, and fetched their seven little candles, so that they might see her the better, and they were so pleased with her beauty that they let her sleep on all night. When the sun rose Snow-White awoke, and, oh! how frightened she was when she saw the seven little dwarfs. But they were very friendly, and asked what her name was. "My name is Snow-White," she answered.

"And how did you come to get into our house?" asked the dwarfs.

Then she told them how her cruel step-mother had intended her to be killed, but how the huntsman had spared her life and she had run on until she reached the little house. And the dwarfs said, "If you will take care of our house, cook for us, make the beds, wash, mend, and knit, and keep everything neat and clean, then you may stay with us altogether and you shall want for nothing."

"With all my heart," answered Snow-White; and so she stayed. She kept the house neat and clean for the dwarfs, who went off early in the morning to search for copper and gold in the mountains, and who expected their meal to be standing ready for them when they returned at night.

All day long Snow-White was alone, and the good little dwarfs warned her to be careful to let no one into the house. "For," said they, "your step-mother will soon discover that you are living here."

The Queen, believing that Snow-White was dead, and that therefore she was again the most beautiful lady in the land, went to her mirror, and said:

"Mirror, mirror upon the wall,
Who is the fairest fair of all?"

Then the mirror answered:

"Lady Queen, though fair ye be,
Snow-White is fairer far to see.
Over the hills and far away,
She dwells with seven dwarfs to-day."

How angry she was, for she knew that the mirror spoke the truth, and that the huntsman must have deceived her. She thought and thought how she might kill Snow-White, for she knew she would have neither rest nor peace until she really was the most beautiful lady in the land. At length she decided what to do. She painted her face and dressed herself like an old pedler-woman, so that no one could recognize her, and in this disguise she climbed the seven mountains that lay between her and the dwarfs' house, and knocked at their door and cried, "Good wares to sell — very cheap to-day!"

Snow-White peeped from the window and said, "Good-day, good wife, what are your wares?"

"All sorts of pretty things, my dear," answered the woman. "Silken laces of every color," and she held up a bright-colored one, made of plaited silks.

"Surely I might let this honest old woman come in?" thought Snow-White, and unbolted the door and bought the pretty lace.

"Dear, dear, what a figure you are," said the old woman; "come, let me lace you properly for once."

Snow-White had no suspicious thoughts, so she placed herself in front of the old woman that she might fasten her dress with the new silk lace. But in less than no time the wicked creature had laced her so tightly that she could not breathe, but fell down upon the ground as though she were dead. "Now," said the Queen, "I am once more the most beautiful lady in the land," and away she went.

When the dwarfs came home they were very grieved to find their dear little Snow-White lying upon the ground as though she were dead. They lifted her gently, and, seeing she was too tightly laced, they cut the silken cord, when she drew a long breath and then gradually came back to life.

When the dwarfs heard all that had happened they said, "The pedler-woman was certainly the wicked Queen. Now, take care in future that you open the door to none when we are not with you."

The wicked Queen had no sooner reached home than she went to her mirror, and said:

"Mirror, mirror upon the wall,
Who is the fairest fair of all?"

And the mirror answered as before:

"O Lady Queen, though fair ye be,
Snow-White is fairer far to see.
Over the hills and far away,
She dwells with seven dwarfs to-day."

The blood rushed to her face as she heard these words, for she knew that Snow-White must have come to life again. "But I will manage to put an end to her yet," she said, and then, by means of her magic, she made a poisonous comb.

Again she disguised herself, climbed the seven mountains, and knocked at the door of the seven dwarfs' cottage, crying, "Good wares to sell — very cheap to-day!" Snow-White looked out of the wrindow and said, "Go away, good woman, for I dare not let you in."

"Surely you can look at my goods," answered the woman, and held up the poisonous comb, which pleased Snow-White so well that she opened the door and bought it.

"Come, let me comb your hair in the newest way," said the woman, but no sooner did the comb touch her hair than the poison began to work, and she fell fainting to the ground. "There, you model of beauty," said the wicked woman, as she went away, "you are done for at last!"

But fortunately it was almost time for the dwarfs to come home, and as soon as they came in and found Snow-White lying upon the ground they guessed that her step-mother had been there again, and set to work to find out what was wrong.

They soon saw the poisonous comb, and drew it out, and almost immediately Snow-White began to recover, and told them what had happened. Once more they warned her to be on her guard, and to open the door to no one.

When the Queen reached home, she went straight to he mirror and said:

"Mirror, mirror upon the wall,
Who is the fairest fair of all?"

And the mirror answered:

"O Lady Queen, though fair ye be,
Snow-White is fairer far to see.
Over the hills and far away,
She dwells with seven dwarfs to-day."

When the Queen heard these words she shook with rage. "Snow-White shall die," she cried, "even if it costs me my own life to manage it."

She went into a secret chamber, where no one else ever entered, and there she made a poisonous apple, and then she painted her face and disguised herself as a peasant woman, and climbed the seven mountains and went to the dwarfs' house.

She knocked at the door. Snow-White looked out of the window, and said, "I must not let any one in; the seven dwarfs have forbidden me to do so."

"It's all the same to me," answered the peasant woman; "I shall soon get rid of these fine apples. But before I go I'll make you a present of one."

"Oh! no," said Snow-White, "for I must not take it."

"Surely you are not afraid of poison?" said the woman. "See, I will cut one in two: the rosy cheek you shall take, and the white cheek I will eat myself."

Now, the apple had been so cleverly made that only the rosy-cheeked side contained the poison. Snow-White longed for the delicious-looking fruit, and when she saw that the woman ate half of it, she thought there could be no danger, and stretched out her hand and took the other part. But no sooner had she tasted it than she fell down dead.

The wicked Queen laughed aloud with joy as she gazed at her. "White as snow, red as blood, black as ebony," she said, "this time the dwarfs cannot awaken you."

And she went home and asked her mirror:

"Mirror, mirror upon the wall,
Who is the fairest fair of all?"

And at length it answered:

"Thou, O Queen, art fairest of all!"

So her envious heart had peace at least, so much peace as an envious heart can have.

When the little dwarfs came home at night they found Snow-White lying upon the ground. No breath came from her parted lips, for she was dead. They lifted her tenderly and sought for some poisonous object which might have caused the mischief, unlaced her frock, combed her hair, and washed her with wine and water, but all in vain—dead she was and dead she remained. They laid her upon a bier, and all seven of them wept as though their hearts would break, for three whole days.

When the time came that she should be laid in the ground they could not bear to part from her. Her pretty cheeks were still rosy red, and she looked just as though she were still living.

"We cannot hide her away in the dark earth," said the dwarfs, and so they made a transparent coffin of shining glass, and laid her in it, and wrote her name upon it in letters of gold; also they wrote that she was a King's daughter. Then they placed the coffin upon the mountain-top, and took turns to watch beside it. And all the animals came and wept for little Snow-White, first an owl, then a raven, and then a little dove.

For a long, long time little Snow-White lay in the coffin, but her form did not wither; she looked as though she slept, for she was still as white as snow, as red as blood, and as black as ebony.

It chanced that a King's son came into the wood; and went to the dwarfs' house, meaning to spend the night there. He saw the coffin upon the mountaintop, with little Snow-White lying within it, and he read the words that were written upon it in letters of gold.

And he said to the dwarfs, "If you will but let me have the coffin, you may ask of me what you will, and I will give it to you." But the dwarfs answered, "We would not sell it for all the gold in the world." Then said the Prince, "Let me have it as a gift, I pray you, for I cannot live without seeing little Snow-White, and I will prize your gift as the dearest of my possessions."

The good little dwarfs pitied him when they heard these words, and so gave him the coffin. The King's son then bade his servants place it upon their shoulders and carry it away, but as they went they stumbled over the stump of a tree, and the violent shaking shook the piece of poisonous apple which had lodged in Snow-White's throat out again, so that she opened her eyes, raised the lid of the coffin, and sat up, alive once more.

"Where am I?" she cried, and the happy Prince answered, "Thou art with me, dearest."

Then he told her all that had happened, and how he loved her better than the whole wide world, and begged her to go with him to his father's palace and be his wife. Snow-White consented, and went with him, and the wedding was celebrated with great splendor and magnificence.

Little Snow-White's wicked step-mother was bidden to the feast, and when she had arrayed herself in her most beautiful garments, she stood before her mirror, and said:

"Mirror, mirror upon the wall,
Who is the fairest fair of all?"

And the mirror answered:

"Oh Lady Queen, though fair ye be,
The young Queen is fairer far to see."

Oh! how angry the wicked woman was then, and so terrified, too, that she scarcely knew what to do. At first she thought she would not go to the wedding at all, but then she felt that she could not rest until she had seen the young Queen. No sooner did she enter the palace than she recognized little Snow-White, and could not move for terror.

Then a pair of red-hot iron shoes was brought into the room with tongs and set down before her, and these she was forced to put on and to dance in them until she could dance no longer, but fell down dead, and there was an end of her.

The Sleeping Beauty in the Wood
Charles Perrault

There were formerly a king and a queen, who were so sorry that they had no children; so sorry that it cannot be expressed. They went to all the waters in the world; vows, pilgrimages, all ways were tried, and all to no purpose.

At last, however, the Queen had a daughter. There was a very fine christening; and the Princess had for her god-mothers all the fairies they could find in the whole kingdom (they found seven), that every one of them might give her a gift, as was the custom of fairies in those days. By this means the Princess had all the perfections imaginable.

After the ceremonies of the christening were over, all the company returned to the King's palace, where was prepared a great feast for the fairies. There was placed before every one of them a magnificent cover with a case of massive gold, wherein were a spoon, knife, and fork, all of pure gold set with diamonds and rubies. But as they were all sitting down at table they saw come into the hall a very old fairy, whom they had not invited, because it was above fifty years since she had been out of a certain tower, and she was believed to be either dead or enchanted.

The King ordered her a cover, but could not furnish her with a case of gold as the others, because they had seven only made for the seven fairies. The old Fairy fancied she was slighted, and muttered some threats between her teeth. One of the young fairies who sat by her overheard how she grumbled; and, judging that she might give the little Princess some unlucky gift, went, as soon as they rose from table, and hid herself behind the hangings, that she might speak last and repair, as much as she could, the evil which the old Fairy might intend.

In the meanwhile all the fairies began to give their gifts to the Princess. The youngest gave her for gift that she should be the most beautiful person in the world; the next, that she should have the wit of an angel; the third, that she should have a wonderful grace in everything she did; the fourth, that she should dance perfectly well; the fifth, that she should sing like a nightingale; and the sixth, that she should play all kinds of music to the utmost perfection.

The old Fairy's turn coming next, with a head shaking more with spite than age, she said that the Princess should have her hand pierced with a spindle and die of the wound. This terrible gift made the whole company tremble, and everybody fell a-crying. At this very instant the young Fairy came out from behind the hangings, and spake these words aloud:

"Assure yourselves, O King and Queen, that your daughter shall not die of this disaster. It is true, I have no power to undo entirely what my elder has done. The Princess shall indeed pierce her hand with a spindle; but, instead of dying, she shall only fall into a profound sleep, which shall last a hundred years, at the expiration of which a king's son shall come and awake her."

The King, to avoid the misfortune foretold by the old Fairy, caused immediately proclamation to be made, whereby everybody was forbidden, on pain of death, to spin with a distaff and spindle, or to have so much as any spindle in their houses. About fifteen or sixteen years after, the King and Queen being gone to one of their houses of pleasure, the young Princess happened one day to divert herself in running up and down the palace; when going up from one apartment to another, she came into a little room on the top of the tower, where a good old woman, alone, was spinning with her spindle. This good woman had never heard of the King's proclamation against spindles.

"What are you doing there, goody?" said the Princess.

"I am spinning, my pretty child," said the old woman, who did not know who she was.

"Ha!" said the Princess, "this is very pretty; how do you do it? Give it to me, that I may see if I can do so."

She had no sooner taken it into her hand than, whether being very hasty at it, somewhat unhandy, or that the decree of the Fairy had so ordained it, it ran into her hand, and she fell down in a swoon.

The good old woman, not knowing very well what to do in this affair, cried out for help. People came in from every quarter in great numbers; they threw water upon the Princess's face, unlaced her, struck her on the palms of her hands, and rubbed her temples with Hungary-water; but nothing would bring her to herself.

And now the King, who came up at the noise, bethought himself of the prediction of the fairies, and, judging very well that this must necessarily come to pass, since the fairies had said it, caused the Princess to be carried into the finest apartment in his palace, and to be laid upon a bed all embroidered with gold and silver.

One would have taken her for a little angel, she was so very beautiful; for her swooning away had not diminished one bit of her complexion: her cheeks were carnation, and her lips were coral; indeed her eyes were shut, but she was heard to breathe softly, which satisfied those about her that she was not dead. The King commanded that they should not disturb her, but let her sleep quietly till her hour of awaking was come.

The good Fairy who had saved her life by condemning her to sleep a hundred years was in the kingdom of Matakin, twelve thousand leagues off, when this accident befell the Princess; but she was instantly informed of it by a little dwarf, who had boots of seven leagues, that is, boots with which he could tread over seven leagues of ground in one stride. The Fairy came away immediately, and she arrived, about an hour after, in a fiery chariot drawn by dragons.

The King handed her out of the chariot, and she approved every thing he had done; but as she had very great foresight, she thought when the Princess should awake she might not know what to do with herself, being all alone in this old palace; and this was what she did: she touched with her wand everything in the palace (except the King and the Queen)—governesses, maids of honour, ladies of the bedchamber, gentlemen, officers, stewards, cooks, undercooks, scullions, guards, with their beefeaters, pages, footmen; she likewise touched all the horses which were in the stables, as well pads as others, the great dogs in the outward court and pretty little Mopsey too, the Princess's little spaniel, which lay by her on the bed.

Immediately upon her touching them they all fell asleep, that they might not awake before their mistress, and that they might be ready to wait upon her when she wanted them. The very spits at the fire, as full as they could hold of partridges and pheasants, did fall asleep also. All this was done in a moment. Fairies are not long in doing their business.

And now the King and the Queen, having kissed their dear child without waking her, went out of the palace and put forth a proclamation that nobody should dare to come near it.

This, however, was not necessary, for in a quarter of an hour's time there grew up all round about the park such a vast number of trees, great and small, bushes and brambles, twining one within another, that neither man nor beast could pass through; so that nothing could be seen but the very top of the towers of the palace; and that, too, not unless it was a good way off. Nobody doubted but the Fairy gave herein a very extraordinary sample of her art, that the Princess, while she continued sleeping, might have nothing to fear from any curious people.

When a hundred years were gone and passed the son of the King then reigning, and who was of another family from that of the sleeping Princess, being gone a-hunting on that side of the country, asked:

What those towers were which he saw in the middle of a great thick wood?

Everyone answered according as they had heard. Some said:

That it was a ruinous old castle, haunted by spirits;

Others, That all the sorcerers and witches of the country kept there their sabbath or nights meeting.

The common opinion was: That an ogre lived there, and that he carried thither all the little children he could catch, that he might eat them up at his leisure, without anybody being able to follow him, as having himself only the power to pass through the wood.

The Prince was at a stand, not knowing what to believe, when a very aged countryman spake to him thus:

"May it please your royal highness, it is now about fifty years since I heard from my father, who heard my grandfather say, that there was then in this castle a princess, the most beautiful was ever seen; that she must sleep there a hundred years, and should be waked by a king's son, for whom she was reserved."

The young Prince was all on fire at these words, believing, without weighing the matter, that he could put an end to this rare adventure; and, pushed on by love and honour, resolved that moment to look into it.

Scarce had he advanced towards the wood when all the great trees, the bushes, and brambles gave way of themselves to let him pass through; he walked up to the castle which he saw at the end of a large avenue which he went into; and what a little surprised him was that he saw none of his people could follow him, because the trees closed again as soon as he had passed through them. However, he did not cease from continuing his way; a young and amorous prince is always valiant.

He came into a spacious outward court, where everything he saw might have frozen up the most fearless person with horror. There reigned over all a most frightful silence; the image of death everywhere showed itself, and there was nothing to be seen but stretched-out bodies of men and animals, all seeming to be dead. He, however, very well knew, by the ruby faces and pimpled noses of the beefeaters, that they were only asleep; and their goblets, wherein still remained some drops of wine, showed plainly that they fell asleep in their cups.

He then crossed a court paved with marble, went up the stairs, and came into the guard chamber, where guards were standing in their ranks, with their muskets upon their shoulders, and snoring as loud as they could. After that he went through several rooms full of gentlemen and ladies, all asleep, some standing, others sitting. At last he came into a chamber all gilded with gold, where he saw upon a bed, the curtains of which were all open, the finest sight was ever beheld — a princess, who appeared to be about fifteen or sixteen years of age, and whose bright and, in a manner, resplendent beauty, had somewhat in it divine. He approached with trembling and admiration, and fell down before her upon his knees.

And now, as the enchantment was at an end, the Princess awaked, and looking on him with eyes more tender than the first view might seem to admit of:

"Is it you, my Prince?" said she to him. "You have waited a long while."

The Prince, charmed with these words, and much more with the manner in which they were spoken, knew not how to show his joy and gratitude; he assured her that he loved her better than he did himself; their discourse was not well connected, they did weep more than talk—little eloquence, a great deal of love. He was more at a loss than she, and we need not wonder at it: she had time to think on what to say to him; for it is very probable (though history mentions nothing of it) that the good Fairy, during so long a sleep, had given her very agreeable dreams. In short, they talked four hours together, and yet they said not half what they had to say.

In the meanwhile all the palace awaked; everyone thought upon their particular business, and as all of them were not in love they were ready to die for hunger. The chief lady of honour, being as sharp set as other folks, grew very impatient, and told the Princess aloud that supper was served up. The Prince helped the Princess to rise; she was entirely dressed, and very magnificently, but his royal highness took care not to tell her that she was dressed like his great-grandmother, and had a point band peeping over a high collar; she looked not a bit the less charming and beautiful for all that.

They went into the great hall of looking-glasses, where they supped, and were served by the Princess's officers; the violins and hautboys played old tunes, but very excellent, though it was now above a hundred years since they had played; and after supper, without losing any time, the lord almoner married them in the chapel of the castle, and the chief lady of honour drew the curtains. They had but very little sleep—the Princess had no occasion; and the Prince left her next morning to return into the city, where his father must needs have been in pain for him. The Prince told him:

That he lost his way in the forest as he was hunting, and that he had lain in the cottage of a charcoal-burner, who gave him cheese and brown bread.

The King, his father, who was a good man, believed him; but his mother could not be persuaded it was true; and seeing that he went almost every day a-hunting, and that he always had some excuse ready for so doing, though he had lain out three or four nights together, she began to suspect that he was married, for he lived with the Princess above two whole years, and had by her two children, the eldest of which, who was a daughter, was named Morning, and the youngest, who was a son, they called Day, because he was a great deal handsomer and more beautiful than his sister.

The Queen spoke several times to her son, to inform herself after what manner he did pass his time, and that in this he ought in duty to satisfy her. But he never dared to trust her with his secret; he feared her, though he loved her, for she was of the race of the ogres, and the King would never have married her had it not been for her vast riches; it was even whispered about the Court that she had Ogreish inclinations, and that, whenever she saw little children passing by, she had all the difficulty in the world to avoid falling upon them. And so the Prince would never tell her one word.

But when the King was dead, which happened about two years afterwards, and he saw himself lord and master, he openly declared his marriage; and he went in great ceremony to conduct his Queen to the palace. They made a magnificent entry into the capital city, she riding between her two children.

Soon after the King went to make war with the Emperor Contalabutte, his neighbour. He left the government of the kingdom to the Queen his mother, and earnestly recommended to her care his wife and children. He was obliged to continue his expedition all the summer, and as soon as he departed the Queen-mother sent her daughter-in-law to a country house among the woods, that she might with the more ease gratify her horrible longing.

Some few days afterwards she went thither herself, and said to her clerk of the kitchen:

"I have a mind to eat little Morning for my dinner to-morrow." "Ah! madam," cried the clerk of the kitchen.

"I will have it so," replied the Queen (and this she spoke in the tone of an ogress who had a strong desire to eat fresh meat), "and will eat her with a sauce Robert."

The poor man, knowing very well that he must not play tricks with ogresses, took his great knife and went up into little Morning's chamber. She was then four years old, and came up to him jumping and laughing, to take him about the neck, and ask him for some sugar-candy. Upon which he began to weep, the great knife fell out of his hand, and he went into the back yard, and killed a little lamb, and dressed it with such good sauce that his mistress assured him she had never eaten anything so good in her life. He had at the same time taken up little Morning, and carried her to his wife, to conceal her in the lodging he had at the bottom of the courtyard.

About eight days afterwards the wicked Queen said to the clerk of the kitchen, "I will sup upon little Day."

He answered not a word, being resolved to cheat her as he had done before. He went to find out little Day, and saw him with a little foil in his hand, with which he was fencing with a great monkey, the child being then only three years of age. He took him up in his arms and carried him to his wife, that she might conceal him in her chamber along with his sister, and in the room of little Day cooked up a young kid, very tender, which the Ogress found to be wonderfully good.

This was hitherto all mighty well; but one evening this wicked Queen said to her clerk of the kitchen:

"I will eat the Queen with the same sauce I had with her children."

It was now that the poor clerk of the kitchen despaired of being able to deceive her. The young Queen was turned of twenty, not reckoning the hundred years she had been asleep; and how to find in the yard a beast so firm was what puzzled him. He took then a resolution, that he might save his own life, to cut the Queen's throat; and going up into her chamber, with intent to do it at once, he put himself into as great fury as he could possibly, and came into the young Queen's room with his dagger in his hand. He would not, however, surprise her, but told her, with a great deal of respect, the orders he had received from the Queen-mother.

"Do it; do it" (said she, stretching out her neck). "Execute your orders, and then I shall go and see my children, my poor children, whom I so much and so tenderly loved."

For she thought them dead ever since they had been taken away without her knowledge.

"No, no, madam" (cried the poor clerk of the kitchen, all in tears); "you shall not die, and yet you shall see your children again; but then you must go home with me to my lodgings, where I have concealed them, and I shall deceive the Queen once more, by giving her in your stead a young hind."

Upon this he forthwith conducted her to his chamber, where, leaving her to embrace her children, and cry along with them, he went and dressed a young hind, which the Queen had for her supper, and devoured it with the same appetite as if it had been the young Queen. Exceedingly was she delighted with her cruelty, and she had invented a story to tell the King, at his return, how the mad wolves had eaten up the Queen his wife and her two children.

One evening, as she was, according to her custom, rambling round about the courts and yards of the palace to see if she could smell any fresh meat, she heard, in a ground room, little Day crying, for his mamma was going to whip him, because he had been naughty; and she heard, at the same time, little Morning begging pardon for her brother.

The ogress presently knew the voice of the Queen and her children, and being quite mad that she had been thus deceived, she commanded next morning, by break of day (with a most horrible voice, which made everybody tremble), that they should bring into the middle of the great court a large tub, which she caused to be filled with toads, vipers, snakes, and all sorts of serpents, in order to have thrown into it the Queen and her children, the clerk of the kitchen, his wife and maid; all whom she had given orders should be brought thither with their hands tied behind them.

They were brought out accordingly, and the executioners were just going to throw them into the tub, when the King (who was not so soon expected) entered the court on horseback (for he came post) and asked, with the utmost astonishment, what was the meaning of that horrible spectacle.

No one dared to tell him, when the ogress, all enraged to see what had happened, threw herself head foremost into the tub, and was instantly devoured by the ugly creatures she had ordered to be thrown into it for others. The King could not but be very sorry, for she was his mother; but he soon comforted himself with his beautiful wife and his pretty children.

Beauty and the Beast
Madame de Villeneuve

Once upon a time, in a very far-off country, there lived a merchant who had been so fortunate in all his undertakings that he was enormously rich. As he had, however, six sons and six daughters, he found that his money was not too much to let them all have everything they fancied, as they were accustomed to do.

But one day a most unexpected misfortune befell them. Their house caught fire and was speedily burnt to the ground, with all the splendid furniture, the books, pictures, gold, silver, and precious goods it contained; and this was only the beginning of their troubles. Their father, who had until this moment prospered in all ways, suddenly lost every ship he had upon the sea, either by dint of pirates, shipwreck, or fire. Then he heard that his clerks in distant countries, whom he trusted entirely, had proved unfaithful; and at last from great wealth he fell into the direst poverty.

All that he had left was a little house in a desolate place at least a hundred leagues from the town in which he had lived, and to this he was forced to retreat with his children, who were in despair at the idea of leading such a different life. Indeed, the daughters at first hoped that their friends, who had been so numerous while they were rich, would insist on their staying in their houses now they no longer possessed one. But they soon found that they were left alone, and that their former friends even attributed their misfortunes to their own extravagance, and showed no intention of offering them any help. So nothing was left for them but to take their departure to the cottage, which stood in the midst of a dark forest, and seemed to be the most dismal place upon the face of the earth. As they were too poor to have any servants, the girls had to work hard, like peasants, and the sons, for their part, cultivated the fields to earn their living. Roughly clothed, and living in the simplest way, the girls regretted unceasingly the luxuries and amusements of their former life; only the youngest tried to be brave and cheerful. She had been as sad as anyone when misfortune first overtook her father, but, soon recovering her natural gaiety, she set to work to make the best of things, to amuse her father and brothers as well as she could, and to try to persuade her sisters to join her in dancing and singing. But they would do nothing of the sort, and, because she was not as doleful as themselves, they declared that this miserable life was all she was fit for. But she was really far prettier and cleverer than they were; indeed, she was so lovely that she was always called Beauty. After two years, when they were all beginning to get used to their new life, something happened to disturb their tranquillity. Their father received the news that one of his ships, which he had believed to be lost, had come safely into port with a rich cargo. All the sons and daughters at once thought that their poverty was at an end, and wanted to set out directly for the town; but their father, who was more prudent, begged them to wait a little, and, though it was harvest.time, and he could ill be spared, determined to go himself first, to make inquiries. Only the youngest daughter had any doubt but that they would soon again be as rich as they were before, or at least rich enough to live comfortably in some town where they would find amusement and gay companions once more. So they all loaded their father with commissions for jewels and dresses which it would have taken a fortune to buy; only Beauty, feeling sure that it was of no use, did not ask for anything. her father, noticing her silence, said: "And what shall I bring for you, Beauty?"

"The only thing I wish for is to see you come home safely," she answered.

But this reply vexed her sisters, who fancied she was blaming them for having asked for such costly things. Her father, however, was pleased, but as he thought that at her age she certainly ought to like pretty presents, he told her to choose something.

"Well, dear father," she said, "as you insist upon it, I beg that you will bring me a rose. I have not seen one since we came here, and I love them so much."

So the merchant set out and reached the town as quickly as possible, but only to find that his former companions, believing him to be dead, had divided between them the goods which the ship had brought; and after six months of trouble and expense he found himself as poor as when he started, having been able to recover only just enough to pay the cost of his journey. To make matters worse, he was obliged to leave the town in the most terrible weather, so that by the time he was within a few leagues of his home he was almost exhausted with cold and fatigue. Though he knew it would take some hours to get through the forest, he was so anxious to be at his journey's end that he resolved to go on; but night overtook him, and the deep snow and bitter frost made it impossible for his horse to carry him any further. Not a house was to be seen; the only shelter he could get was the hollow trunk of a great tree, and there he crouched all the night, which seemed to him the longest he had ever known. In spite of his weariness the howling of the wolves kept him awake, and even when at last the day broke he was not much better off, for the falling snow had covered up every path, and he did not know which way to turn.

At length he made out some sort of track, and though at the beginning it was so rough and slippery that he fell down more than once, it presently became easier, and led him into an avenue of trees which ended in a splendid castle. It seemed to the merchant very strange that no snow had fallen in the avenue, which was entirely composed of orange trees, covered with flowers and fruit. When he reached the first court of the castle he saw before him a flight of agate steps, and went up them, and passed through several splendidly furnished rooms. The pleasant warmth of the air revived him, and he felt very hungry; but there seemed to be nobody in all this vast and splendid palace whom he could ask to give him something to eat. Deep silence reigned everywhere, and at last, tired of roaming through empty rooms and galleries, he stopped in a room smaller than the rest, where a clear fire was burning and a couch was drawn up cosily close to it. Thinking that this must be prepared for someone who was expected, he sat down to wait till he should come, and very soon fell into a sweet sleep.

When his extreme hunger wakened him after several hours, he was still alone; but a little table, upon which was a good dinner, had been drawn up close to him, and, as he had eaten nothing for twenty-four hours, he lost no time in beginning his meal, hoping that he might soon have an opportunity of thanking his considerate entertainer, whoever it might be. But no one appeared, and even after another long sleep, from which he awoke completely refreshed, there was no sign of anybody, though a fresh meal of dainty cakes and fruit was prepared upon the little table at his elbow. Being naturally timid, the silence began to terrify him, and he resolved to search once more through all the rooms; but it was of no use. Not even a servant was to be seen; there was no sign of life in the palace! He began to wonder what he should do, and to amuse himself by pretending that all the treasures he saw were his own, and considering how he would divide them among his children. Then he went down into the garden, and though it was winter everywhere else, here the sun shone, and the birds sang, and the flowers bloomed, and the air was soft and sweet. The merchant, in ecstacies with all he saw and heard, said to himself:

"All this must be meant for me. I will go this minute and bring my children to share all these delights."

In spite of being so cold and weary when he reached the castle, he had taken his horse to the stable and fed it. Now he thought he would saddle it for his homeward journey, and he turned down the path which led to the stable. This path had a hedge of roses on each side of it, and the merchant thought he had never seen or smelt such exquisite flowers. They reminded him of his promise to Beauty, and he stopped and had just gathered one to take to her when he was startled by a strange noise behind him. Turning round, he saw a frightful Beast, which seemed to be very angry and said, in a terrible voice:

"Who told you that you might gather my roses? Was it not enough that I allowed you to be in my palace and was kind to you? This is the way you show your gratitude, by stealing my flowers! But your insolence shall not go unpunished." The merchant, terrified by these furious words, dropped the fatal rose, and, throwing himself on his knees, cried: "Pardon me, noble sir. I am truly grateful to you for your hospitality, which was so magnificent that I could not imagine that you would be offended by my taking such a little thing as a rose." But the Beast's anger was not lessened by this speech.

"You are very ready with excuses and flattery," he cried; "but that will not save you from the death you deserve."

"Alas!" thought the merchant, "if my daughter Beauty could only know what danger her rose has brought me into!"

And in despair he began to tell the Beast all his misfortunes, and the reason of his journey, not forgetting to mention Beauty's request.

"A king's ransom would hardly have procured all that my other daughters asked," he said; "but I thought that I might at least take Beauty her rose. I beg you to forgive me, for you see I meant no harm."

The Beast considered for a moment, and then he said, in a less furious tone:

"I will forgive you on one condition—that is, that you will give me one of your daughters."

"Ah!" cried the merchant, "if I were cruel enough to buy my own life at the expense of one of my children's, what excuse could I invent to bring her here?"

"No excuse would be necessary," answered the Beast. "If she comes at all she must come willingly. On no other condition will I have her. See if any one of them is courageous enough, and loves you well enough to come and save your life. You seem to be an honest man, so I will trust you to go home. I give you a month to see if either of your daughters will come back with you and stay here, to let you go free. If neither of them is willing, you must come alone, after bidding them good-bye for ever, for then you will belong to me. And do not imagine that you can hide from me, for if you fail to keep your word I will come and fetch you!" added the Beast grimly.

The merchant accepted this proposal, though he did not really think any of his daughters would be persuaded to come. He promised to return at the time appointed, and then, anxious to escape from the presence of the Beast, he asked permission to set off at once. But the Beast answered that he could not go until the next day.

"Then you will find a horse ready for you," he said. "Now go and eat your supper, and await my orders."

The poor merchant, more dead than alive, went back to his room, where the most delicious supper was already served on the little table which was drawn up before a blazing fire. But he was too terrified to eat, and only tasted a few of the dishes, for fear the Beast should be angry if he did not obey his orders. When he had finished he heard a great noise in the next room, which he knew meant that the Beast was coming. As he could do nothing to escape his visit, the only thing that remained was to seem as little afraid as possible; so when the Beast appeared and asked roughly if he had supped well, the merchant answered humbly that he had, thanks to his host's kindness. Then the Beast warned him to remember their agreement, and to prepare his daughter exactly for what she had to expect.

"Do not get up tomorrow," he added, "until you see the sun and hear a golden bell ring. Then you will find your breakfast waiting for you here, and the horse you are to ride will be ready in the courtyard. He will also bring you back again when you come with your daughter a month hence. Farewell. Take a rose to Beauty, and remember your promise!"

The merchant was only too glad when the Beast went away, and though he could not sleep for sadness, he lay down until the sun rose. Then, after a hasty breakfast, he went to gather Beauty's rose, and mounted his horse, which carried him off so swiftly that in an instant he had lost sight of the palace, and he was still wrapped in gloomy thoughts when it stopped before the door of the cottage.

His sons and daughters, who had been very uneasy at his long absence, rushed to meet him, eager to know the result of his journey, which, seeing him mounted upon a splendid horse and wrapped in a rich mantle, they supposed to be favourable. But he hid the truth from them at first, only saying sadly to Beauty as he gave her the rose:

"Here is what you asked me to bring you; you little know what it has cost."

But this excited their curiosity so greatly that presently he told them his adventures from beginning to end, and then they were all very unhappy. The girls lamented loudly over their lost hopes, and the sons declared that their father should not return to this terrible castle, and began to make plans for killing the Beast if it should come to fetch him. But he reminded them that he had promised to go back. Then the girls were very angry with Beauty, and said it was all her fault, and that if she had asked for some thing sensible this would never have happened, and complained bitterly that they should have to suffer for her folly.

Poor Beauty, much distressed, said to them:

"I have indeed caused this misfortune, but I assure you I did it inno-
cently. Who could have guessed that to ask for a rose in the middle of
summer would cause so much misery? But as I did the mischief it is only
just that I should suffer for it. I will therefore go back with my father to
keep his promise."

At first nobody would hear of this arrangement, and her father and
brothers, who loved her dearly, declared that nothing should make them
let her go; but Beauty was firm. As the time drew near she divided all
her little possessions between her sisters, and said goodbye to everything
she loved, and when the fatal day came she encouraged and cheered her
father as they mounted together the horse which had brought him back.
It seemed to fly rather than gallop, but so smoothly that Beauty was
not frightened; indeed, she would have enjoyed the journey if she had
not feared what might happen to her at the end of it. Her father still
tried to persuade her to go back, but in vain. While they were talking
the night fell, and then, to their great surprise, wonderful coloured lights
began to shine in all directions, and splendid fireworks blazed on before
them; all the forest was illuminated by them, and even felt pleasantly
warm, though it had been bitterly cold before. This lasted until they
reached the avenue of orange trees, where were statues holding flaming
torches, and when they got nearer to the palace they saw that it was
illuminated from the roof to the ground, and music sounded softly from
the courtyard. "The Beast must be very hungry," said Beauty, trying to
laugh, "if he makes all this rejoicing over the arrival of his prey."

But, in spite of her anxiety, she could not help admiring all the wonderful things she saw.

The horse stopped at the foot of the flight of steps leading to the
terrace, and when they had dismounted her father led her to the little
room he had been in before, where they found a splendid fire burning,
and the table daintily spread with a delicious supper.

The merchant knew that this was meant for them, and Beauty, who
was rather less frightened now that she had passed through so many
rooms and seen nothing of the Beast, was quite willing to begin, for her
long ride had made her very hungry. But they had hardly finished their
meal when the noise of the Beast's footsteps was heard approaching, and
Beauty clung to her father in terror, which became all the greater when
she saw how frightened he was. But when the Beast really appeared,
though she trembled at the sight of him, she made a great effort to hide
her horror, and saluted him respectfully.

This evidently pleased the Beast. After looking at her he said, in a
tone that might have struck terror into the boldest heart, though he did
not seem to be angry:

"Good-evening, old man. Good-evening, Beauty."

The merchant was too terrified to reply, but Beauty answered sweetly: "Good-evening, Beast."

"Have you come willingly?" asked the Beast. "Will you be content to stay here when your father goes away?"

Beauty answered bravely that she was quite prepared to stay.

"I am pleased with you," said the Beast. "As you have come of your own accord, you may stay. As for you, old man," he added, turning to the merchant, "at sunrise to-morrow you will take your departure. When the bell rings get up quickly and eat your breakfast, and you will find the same horse waiting to take you home; but remember that you must never expect to see my palace again."

Then turning to Beauty, he said:

"Take your father into the next room, and help him to choose everything you think your brothers and sisters would like to have. You will find two travelling-trunks there; fill them as full as you can. It is only just that you should send them something very precious as a remembrance of yourself."

Then he went away, after saying, "Good-bye, Beauty; good-bye, old man;" and though Beauty was beginning to think with great dismay of her father's departure, she was afraid to disobey the Beast's orders; and they went into the next room, which had shelves and cupboards all round it. They were greatly surprised at the riches it contained. There were splendid dresses fit for a queen, with all the ornaments that were to be worn with them; and when Beauty opened the cupboards she was quite dazzled by the gorgeous jewels that lay in heaps upon every shelf. After choosing a vast quantity, which she divided between her sisters–for she had made a heap of the wonderful dresses for each of them — she opened the last chest, which was full of gold.

"I think, father," she said, "that, as the gold will be more useful to you, we had better take out the other things again, and fill the trunks with it." So they did this; but the more they put in, the more room there seemed to be, and at last they put back all the jewels and dresses they had taken out, and Beauty even added as many more of the jewels as she could carry at once; and then the trunks were not too full, but they were so heavy that an elephant could not have carried them.

"The Beast was mocking us," cried the merchant; "he must have pretended to give us all these things, knowing that I could not carry them away."

"Let us wait and see," answered Beauty. "I cannot believe that he meant to deceive us. All we can do is to fasten them up and leave them ready."

So they did this and returned to the little room, where, to their astonishment, they found breakfast ready. The merchant ate his with a good appetite, as the Beast's generosity made him believe that he might perhaps venture to come back soon and see Beauty. But she felt sure that her father was leaving her for ever, so she was very sad when the bell rang sharply for the second time, and warned them that the time was come for them to part. They went down into the courtyard, where two horses were waiting, one loaded with the two trunks, the other for him to ride. They were pawing the ground in their impatience to start, and the merchant was forced to bid Beauty a hasty farewell; and as soon as he was mounted he went off at such a pace that she lost sight of him in an instant. Then Beauty began to cry, and wandered sadly back to her own room. But she soon found that she was very sleepy, and as she had nothing better to do she lay down and instantly fell asleep. And then she dreamed that she was walking by a brook bordered with trees, and lamenting her sad fate, when a young prince, handsomer than anyone she had ever seen, and with a voice that went straight to her heart, came and said to her, "Ah, Beauty! you are not so unfortunate as you suppose. Here you will be rewarded for all you have suffered elsewhere. Your every wish shall be gratified. Only try to find me out, no matter how I may be disguised, as I love you dearly, and in making me happy you will find your own happiness. Be as true-hearted as you are beautiful, and we shall have nothing left to wish for."

"What can I do, Prince, to make you happy?" said Beauty.

"Only be grateful," he answered, "and do not trust too much to your eyes. And, above all, do not desert me until you have saved me from my cruel misery."

After this she thought she found herself in a room with a stately and beautiful lady, who said to her:

"Dear Beauty, try not to regret all you have left behind you, for you are destined to a better fate. Only do not let yourself be deceived by appearances."

Beauty found her dreams so interesting that she was in no hurry to awake, but presently the clock roused her by calling her name softly twelve times, and then she got up and found her dressing-table set out with everything she could possibly want; and when her toilet was finished she found dinner was waiting in the room next to hers. But dinner does not take very long when you are all by yourself, and very soon she sat down cosily in the corner of a sofa, and began to think about the charming Prince she had seen in her dream.

"He said I could make him happy," said Beauty to herself.

"It seems, then, that this horrible Beast keeps him a prisoner. How can I set him free? I wonder why they both told me not to trust to appearances? I don't understand it. But, after all, it was only a dream, so why should I trouble myself about it? I had better go and find something to do to amuse myself."

So she got up and began to explore some of the many rooms of the palace.

The first she entered was lined with mirrors, and Beauty saw herself reflected on every side, and thought she had never seen such a charming room. Then a bracelet which was hanging from a chandelier caught her eye, and on taking it down she was greatly surprised to find that it held a portrait of her unknown admirer, just as she had seen him in her dream. With great delight she slipped the bracelet on her arm, and went on into a gallery of pictures, where she soon found a portrait of the same handsome Prince, as large as life, and so well painted that as she studied it he seemed to smile kindly at her. Tearing herself away from the portrait at last, she passed through into a room which contained every musical instrument under the sun, and here she amused herself for a long while in trying some of them, and singing until she was tired. The next room was a library, and she saw everything she had ever wanted to read, as well as everything she had read, and it seemed to her that a whole lifetime would not be enough to read the names of the books, there were so many. By this time it was growing dusk, and wax candles in diamond and ruby candlesticks were beginning to light themselves in every room.

Beauty found her supper served just at the time she preferred to have it, but she did not see anyone or hear a sound, and, though her father had warned her that she would be alone, she began to find it rather dull.

But presently she heard the Beast coming, and wondered tremblingly if he meant to eat her up now.

However, as he did not seem at all ferocious, and only said gruffly:

"Good evening, Beauty," she answered cheerfully and managed to conceal her terror. Then the Beast asked her how she had been and Beauty answered that everything was so beautiful that she would be very hard to please if she could not be happy. And after about an hour's talk Beauty began to think that the Beast was not nearly so terrible as she had supposed at first. Then he got up to leave her, and said in his gruff voice:

"Do you love me, Beauty? Will you marry me?"

"Oh! what shall I say?" cried Beauty, for she was afraid to make the Beast angry by refusing.

"Say 'yes' or 'no' without fear," he replied.

"Oh! no, Beast," said Beauty hastily.

"Since you will not, good-night, Beauty," he said. And she answered:

"Good-night, Beast," very glad to find that her refusal had not provoked him. And after he was gone she was very soon in bed and asleep, and dreaming of her unknown Prince. She thought he came and said to her:

"Ah, Beauty! why are you so unkind to me? I fear I am fated to be unhappy for many a long day still."

And then her dreams changed, but the charming Prince figured in them all; and when morning came her first thought was to look at the portrait and see if it was really like him, and she found that it certainly was.

This morning she decided to amuse herself in the garden, for the sun shone, and all the fountains were playing; but she was astonished to find that every place was familiar to her, and presently she came to the brook where the myrtle trees were growing where she had first met the Prince in her dream, and that made her think more than ever that he must be kept a prisoner by the Beast. When she was tired she went back to the palace, and found a new room full of materials for every kind of work — ribbons to make into bows, and silks to work into flowers. Then there was an aviary full of rare birds, which were so tame that they flew to Beauty as soon as they saw her, and perched upon her shoulders and her head.

"Pretty little creatures," she said, "how I wish that your cage was nearer to my room, that I might often hear you sing!"

So saying she opened a door, and found to her delight that it led into her own room, though she had thought it was quite the other side of the palace.

There were more birds in a room farther on, parrots and cockatoos that could talk, and they greeted Beauty by name; indeed, she found them so entertaining that she took one or two back to her room, and they talked to her while she was at supper; after which the Beast paid her his usual visit, and asked the same questions as before, and then with a gruff 'good-night' he took his departure, and Beauty went to bed to dream of her mysterious Prince. The days passed swiftly in different amusements, and after a while Beauty found out another strange thing in the palace, which often pleased her when she was tired of being alone. There was one room which she had not noticed particularly; it was empty, except that under each of the windows stood a very comfortable chair; and the first time she had looked out of the window it had seemed to her that a black curtain prevented her from seeing anything outside. But the second time she went into the room, happening to be tired, she sat down in one of the chairs, when instantly the curtain was rolled aside, and a most amusing pantomime was acted before her; there were dancers, and coloured lights, and music, and pretty dresses, and it was all so gay that Beauty was in ecstacies. After that she tried the other seven windows in turn, and there was some new and surprising entertainment to be seen from each of them, so that Beauty never could feel lonely anymore. Every evening after supper the Beast came to see her, and always before saying good-night asked her in his terrible voice:

"Beauty, will you marry me?"

And it seemed to Beauty, now she understood him better, that when she said, "No, Beast," he went away quite sad. But her happy dreams of the handsome young Prince soon made her forget the poor Beast, and the only thing that at all disturbed her was to be constantly told to distrust appearances, to let her heart guide her, consider as she would, she could not understand.

So everything went on for a long time, until at the last, happy as she was, Beauty began to long for the sight of her father and her brothers and sisters; and one night, seeing her look very sad, the Beast asked her what was the matter. Beauty had quite ceased to be afraid of him. Now she knew that he was really gentle in spite of his ferocious looks and his dreadful voice. So she answered that she was longing to see her home once more. Upon hearing this the Beast seemed sadly distressed, and cried miserably.

"Ah! Beauty, have you the heart to desert an unhappy Beast like this? What more do you want to make you happy? Is it because you hate me that you want to escape?"

"No, dear Beast," answered Beauty softly, "I do not hate you, and I should be very sorry never to see you any more, but I long to see my father again. Only let me go for two months, and I promise to come back to you and stay for the rest of my life."

The Beast, who had been sighing dolefully while she spoke, now replied:

"I cannot refuse you anything you ask, even though it should cost me my life. Take the four boxes you will find in the room next to your own, and fill them with everything you wish to take with you. But remember your promise and come back when the two months are over, or you may have cause to repent it, for if you do not come in good time you will find your faithful Beast dead. You will not need any chariot to bring you back. Only say good-bye to all your brothers and sisters the night before you come away, and when you have gone to bed turn this ring round upon your finger and say firmly: 'I wish to go back to my palace and see my Beast again.' Good-night, Beauty. Fear nothing, sleep peacefully, and before long you shall see your father once more."

As soon as Beauty was alone she hastened to fill the boxes with all the rare and precious things she saw about her, and only when she was tired of heaping things into them did they seem to be full.

Then she went to bed, but could hardly sleep for joy. And when at last she did begin to dream of her beloved Prince she was grieved to see him stretched upon a grassy bank sad and weary, and hardly like himself.

"What is the matter?" she cried.

But he looked at her reproachfully, and said:

"How can you ask me, cruel one? Are you not leaving me to my death perhaps?"

"Ah! don't be so sorrowful," cried Beauty; "I am only going to assure my father that I am safe and happy. I have promised the Beast faithfully that I will come back, and he would die of grief if I did not keep my word!"

"What would that matter to you?" said the Prince. "Surely you would not care?"

"Indeed I should be ungrateful if I did not care for such a kind Beast," cried Beauty indignantly. "I would die to save him from pain. I assure you it is not his fault that he is so ugly."

Just then a strange sound woke her-someone was speaking not very far away; and opening her eyes she found herself in a room she had never seen before, which was certainly not nearly so splendid as those she was used to in the Beast's palace. Where could she be? She got up and dressed herself hastily, and then she saw that the boxes she had packed the night before were all in the room. While she was wondering by what magic the Beast had transported them and herself to this strange place she suddenly heard her father's voice, and rushed out and greeted him joyfully. Her brothers and sisters were all astonished at her appearance, as they had never expected to see her again, and there was no end to the questions they asked her. She had also much to hear about what had happened to them while she was away, and of her father's journey home. But when they heard that she had only come to be with them for a short time, and then must go back to the Beast's palace forever, they lamented loudly. Then beauty asked her father what he thought could be the meaning of her strange dreams, and why the Prince constantly begged her not to trust to appearances. After much consideration he answered: "You tell me yourself that the Beast, frightful as he is, loves you dearly, and deserves your love and gratitude for his gentleness and kindness; I think the Prince must mean you to understand that you ought to reward him by doing as he wishes you to, in spite of his ugliness."

Beauty could not help seeing that this seemed very probable; still, when she thought of her dear Prince who was so handsome, she did not feel at all inclined to marry the Beast. At any rate, for two months she need not decide, but could enjoy herself with her sisters. But though they were rich now, and lived in a town again, and had plenty of acquaintances, Beauty found that nothing amused her very much; and she often thought of the palace, where she was so happy, especially as at home she never once dreamed of her dear Prince, and she felt quite sad without him.

Then her sisters seemed to have got quite used to being without her, and even found her rather in the way, so she would not have been sorry when the two months were over but for her father and brothers, who begged her to stay, and seemed so grieved at the thought of her departure that she had not the courage to say good-bye to them. Every day when she got up she meant to say it at night, and when night came she put it off again, until at last she had a dismal dream which helped her to make up her mind. She thought she was wandering in a lonely path in the palace gardens, when she heard groans which seemed to come from some bushes hiding the entrance of a cave, and running quickly to see what could be the matter, she found the Beast stretched out upon his side, apparently dying. He reproached her faintly with being the cause of his distress, and at the same moment a stately lady appeared, and said very gravely:

"Ah! Beauty, you are only just in time to save his life. See what happens when people do not keep their promises! If you had delayed one day more, you would have found him dead."

Beauty was so terrified by this dream that the next morning she announced her intention of going back at once, and that very night she said good-bye to her father and all her brothers and sisters, and as soon as she was in bed she turned her ring round upon her finger, and said firmly:

"I wish to go back to my palace and see my Beast again," as she had been told to do.

Then she fell asleep instantly, and only woke up to hear the clock saying, "Beauty, Beauty," twelve times in its musical voice, which told her at once that she was really in the palace once more. Everything was just as before, and her birds were so glad to see her! but Beauty thought she had never known such a long day, for she was so anxious to see the Beast again that she felt as if suppertime would never come.

But when it did come and no Beast appeared she was really frightened; so, after listening and waiting for a long time, she ran down into the garden to search for him. Up and down the paths and avenues ran poor Beauty, calling him in vain, for no one answered, and not a trace of him could she find; until at last, quite tired, she stopped for a minute's rest, and saw that she was standing opposite the shady path she had seen in her dream. She rushed down it, and, sure enough, there was the cave, and in it lay the Beast — asleep, as Beauty thought. Quite glad to have found him, she ran up and stroked his head, but to her horror he did not move or open his eyes.

"Oh! he is dead; and it is all my fault," said Beauty, crying bitterly.

But then, looking at him again, she fancied he still breathed, and, hastily fetching some water from the nearest fountain, she sprinkled it over his face, and to her great delight he began to revive.

"Oh! Beast, how you frightened me!" she cried. "I never knew how much I loved you until just now, when I feared I was too late to save your life."

"Can you really love such an ugly creature as I am?" said the Beast faintly. "Ah! Beauty, you only came just in time. I was dying because I thought you had forgotten your promise. But go back now and rest, I shall see you again by-and-by."

Beauty, who had half expected that he would be angry with her, was reassured by his gentle voice, and went back to the palace, where supper was awaiting her; and afterwards the Beast came in as usual, and talked about the time she had spent with her father, asking if she had enjoyed herself, and if they had all been very glad to see her.

Beauty answered politely, and quite enjoyed telling him all that had happened to her. And when at last the time came for him to go, and he asked, as he had so often asked before:

"Beauty, will you marry me?" she answered softly:

"Yes, dear Beast."

As she spoke a blaze of light sprang up before the windows of the palace; fireworks crackled and guns banged, and across the avenue of orange trees, in letters all made of fire-flies, was written: 'Long live the Prince and his Bride.'

Turning to ask the Beast what it could all mean, Beauty found that he had disappeared, and in his place stood her long-loved Prince! At the same moment the wheels of a chariot were heard upon the terrace, and two ladies entered the room. One of them Beauty recognized as the stately lady she had seen in her dreams; the other was also so grand and queenly that Beauty hardly knew which to greet first.

But the one she already knew said to her companion:

"Well, Queen, this is Beauty, who has had the courage to rescue your son from the terrible enchantment. They love one another, and only your consent to their marriage is wanting to make them perfectly happy."

"I consent with all my heart," cried the Queen. "How can I ever thank you enough, charming girl, for having restored my dear son to his natural form?"

And then she tenderly embraced Beauty and the Prince, who had meanwhile been greeting the Fairy and receiving her congratulations.

"Now," said the Fairy to Beauty, "I suppose you would like me to send for all your brothers and sisters to dance at your wedding?"

And so she did, and the marriage was celebrated the very next day with the utmost splendour, and Beauty and the Prince lived happily ever after.

The Rose Tree
Jakob and Wilhelm Grimm

Once upon a time, long long years ago, in the days when one had to be careful about witches, there lived a good man, whose young wife died, leaving him a baby girl. Now this good man felt he could not look after the baby properly, so he married a young woman whose husband had died leaving her with a baby boy.

Thus the two children grew up together, and loved each other dearly.

But the boy's mother was really a wicked witch-woman, and so jealous that she wanted all the boy's love for herself, and when the girl-baby grew white as milk, with cheeks like roses and lips like cherries, and when her hair, shining like golden silk, hung down to her feet so that her father and all the neighbours began to praise her looks, the stepmother fairly hated her, and did all in her power to spoil her looks. She would set the child hard tasks, and send her out in all weathers to do difficult errands, and if they were not well performed would beat her and scold her cruelly.

Now one cold winter evening when the snow was drifting fast, and the wild rose tree in the garden under which the children used to play in summer was all brown and barren save for snowflake flowers, the stepmother said to the little girl:

"Child! go and buy me a bunch of candles at the grocer's. Here is some money; go quickly, and don't loiter on the way."

So the little girl took the money and set off quickly through the snow, for already it was growing dark. Now there was such a wind blowing that it nearly blew her off her feet, and as she ran her beautiful hair got all tangled and almost tripped her up. However, she got the candles, paid for them, and started home again. But this time the wind was behind her and blew all her beautiful golden hair in front of her like a cloud, so that she could not see her steps, and, coming to a stile, had to stop and put down the bundle of candles in order to see how to get over it. And when she was climbing it, a big black, dog came by and ran off with the bunch of candles! Now she was so afraid of her stepmother that she durst not go home, but turned back and bought another bunch of candles at the grocer's, and when she arrived at the stile once more, the same thing happened. A big black dog came down the road and ran away with the bunch of candles. So yet once again she journeyed back to the grocer's through wind and snow, and, with her last penny, bought yet another bunch of candles. To no purpose, for alas! when she laid them down in order to part her beautiful golden hair and to see how to get over the stile, a big black dog ran away with them.

So nothing was left save to go back to her stepmother in fear and trembling. But, for a wonder, her stepmother did not seem very angry. She only scolded her for being so late, for, see you, her father and her little playmate had gone to their beds and were in the Land of Nod.

Then she said to the child, "I must take the tangles out of your hair before you go to sleep. Come, put your head on my lap."

So the little girl put her head on her stepmother's lap, and, lo and behold! her beautiful yellow-silk hair rolled right over the woman's knees and lay upon the ground.

Then the beauty of it made the stepmother more jealous than before, so she said, "I cannot part your hair properly on my knee, fetch me a billet of wood."

So the little girl fetched one. Then said the stepmother, "Your hair is so thick I cannot part it with a comb; fetch me an axe!"

So the child fetched an axe.

"Now," said that wicked, wicked woman, "lay your head down on the billet while I part your hair."

And the child did as she was bid without fear; and lo! the beautiful little golden head was off in a second, by one blow of the axe.

Now the wicked stepmother had thought it all out before, so she took the poor little dead girl out to the garden, dug a hollow in the snow under the rose tree, and said to herself, "When spring comes and the snow melts, if people find her bones, they will say she lost her way and fell asleep in the snow."

But first, because she was a wicked witch-woman, knowing spells and charms, she took out the heart of the little girl and made it into two savoury pies, one for her husband's breakfast and one for the little boy's, for thus would the love they bore to the little girl become hers. Nevertheless, she was mistaken, for when morning came and the little child could not be found, the father sent away his breakfast barely tasted, and the little boy wept so that he could eat nothing.

So they grieved and grieved. And when the snow melted and they found the bones of the poor child, they said, "She must have lost her way that dark night going to the grocer's to buy candles." So they buried the bones under the children's rose tree, and every day the little boy sat there, and wept and wept for his lost playmate.

Now when summer came the wild rose tree flowered. It was covered with white roses, and amongst the flowers there sat a beautiful white bird. And it sang and sang and sang like an angel out of heaven; but what it sang the little boy could never make out, for he could hardly see for weeping, hardly hear for sobbing.

So at last the beautiful white bird unfolded its broad white wings and flew to a cobbler's shop, where a myrtle bush hung over the man and his bench, on which he was making a dainty little pair of rose-red shoes. Then it perched on a bough and sang ever so sweetly:

"Stepmother slew me, Father nigh ate me, He whom I dearly love Sits below, I sing above, Stick! Stock! Stone dead!"

"Sing that beautiful song again," said the cobbler. "It is better than a nightingale's."

"That will I gladly," sang the bird, "if you will give me the little rose-red shoes you are making."

And the cobbler gave them willingly, so the white bird sang its song once more. Then with the rose-red shoes in one foot it flew to an ash tree that grew close beside a goldsmith's bench, and sang:

"Stepmother slew me, Father nigh ate me, He whom I dearly love Sits below, I sing above, Stick! Stock! Stone dead!"

"Oh, what a beautiful song!" cried the goldsmith. "Sing again, dear bird, it is sweeter than a nightingale's."

"That will I gladly," sang the bird, "if you will give me the gold chain you're making."

And the goldsmith gave the bauble willingly, and the bird sang its song once more. Then with the rose-red shoes in one foot and the golden chain in the other, the bird flew to an oak tree which overhung the mill stream, beside which three millers were busy picking out a millstone, and, perching on a bough, sang its song ever so sweetly:

"My stepmother slew me, My father nigh ate me, He whom I dearly love Sits below, I sing above, Stick! — "

Just then one of the millers put down his tool and listened

"Stock!" sang the bird. And the second miller put aside his tool and listened.

"Stone," sang the bird. Then the third miller put aside his tool and listened.

"Dead!" sang the bird so sweetly that with one accord the millers looked up and cried with one voice:

"Oh, what a beautiful song! Sing it again, dear bird, it is sweeter than a nightingale's."

"That will I gladly," answered the bird, "if you will hang the millstone you are picking round my neck."

So the millers hung it as they were asked; and when the song was finished, the bird spread its wide white wings and, with the millstone round its neck and the little rose-red shoes in one foot, the golden chain in the other, it flew back to the rose tree. But the little playmate was not there; he was inside the house eating his dinner.

Then the bird flew to the house, and rattled the millstone about the eaves until the stepmother cried, "Hearken! How it thunders!"

So the little boy ran out to see, and down dropped the dainty rose-red shoes at his feet.

"See what fine things the thunder has brought!" he cried with glee as he ran back.

Then the white bird rattled the millstone about the eaves once more, and once again the stepmother said, "Hearken! How it thunders!"

So this time the father went out to see, and down dropped the golden chain about his neck.

"It is true," he said when he came back. "The thunder does bring fine things!"

Then once more the white bird rattled the millstone about the eaves, and this time the stepmother said hurriedly, "Hark! there it is again! Perhaps it has got something for me!"

Then she ran out; but the moment she stepped outside the door, down fell the millstone right on her head and killed her.

So that was an end of her. And after that the little boy was ever so much happier, and all the summer time he sat with his little rose-coloured shoes under the wild rose tree and listened to the white bird's song. But when winter came and the wild rose tree was all barren and bare save for snowflake flowers, the white bird came no longer and the little boy grew tired of waiting for it. So one day he gave up altogether, and they buried him under the rose tree beside his little playmate.

Now when the spring came and the rose tree blossomed, the flowers were no longer white. They were edged with rose colour like the little boy's shoes, and in the centre of each blossom there was a beautiful tuft of golden silk like the little girl's hair. And if you look in a wild rose you will find these things there still.

The Stone Cutter

A Japanese Tale

Once upon a time there lived a stonecutter who went every day to a great rock in the side of a big mountain and cut out slabs for gravestones or for houses. He understood very well the kinds of stones wanted for the different purposes, and as he was a careful workman he had plenty of customers. For a long time he was quite happy and contented and asked for nothing better than what he had.

Now in the mountain dwelt a spirit which sometimes appeared to men and helped them in many ways to become rich and prosperous. The stonecutter, however, had never seen this spirit and only shook his head, with an unbelieving air, when anyone spoke of it. But a time was coming when he learned to change his opinion.

One day the stonecutter carried a gravestone to the house of a rich man and saw there all sorts of beautiful things, of which he had never even dreamed. Suddenly his daily work seemed to be harder and heavier, and he said to himself:

"Oh, if only I were a rich man, and could sleep in a bed with silken curtains and golden tassels, how happy I should be."

And a voice answered him, "Your wish is heard; a rich man you shall be!" At the sound of the voice the stonecutter looked round but could see nobody. He thought it was all his fancy and picked up his tools and went home, for he did not feel inclined to do any more work that day. But when he reached the little house where he lived, he stood still with amazement, for in place of his wooden hut was a stately palace filled with splendid furniture, and most splendid of all was the bed, in every respect like the one he had envied. He was nearly beside himself with joy, and in his new life the old one was soon forgotten.

It was now the beginning of summer and each day the sun blazed more fiercely. One morning the heat was so great that the stonecutter could scarcely breathe and he determined he would stop at home till the evening.

He was rather dull, for he had never learned how to amuse himself, and was peeping through the closed blinds to see who was going by in the street, when a little carriage passed by drawn by servants dressed in blue and silver. In the carriage sat a prince, and over his head a golden umbrella was held, to protect him from the sun's rays.

"Oh, if I were only a prince," said the stonecutter to himself, as the carriage vanished round the corner. "Oh, if I were only a prince, and could go in such a carriage and have a golden umbrella held over me, how happy I should be!"

And the voice of the mountain spirit answered, "Your wish is heard; a prince you shall be."

And a prince he was. Before his carriage rode one column of men and another behind it. Servants dressed in scarlet and gold bore him along, the coveted umbrella was held over his head, everything his heart could desire was his. But yet it was not enough. He looked round still for something to wish for, and when he saw that in spite of the water he poured on his grass the rays of the sun scorched it, and that in spite of the umbrella held over his head each day his face grew brown and browner, he cried in his anger:

"The sun is mightier than I; oh, if I were only the sun!"

And the mountain spirit answered, "Your wish is heard; the sun you shall be."

And the sun he was, and felt himself proud in his power. He shot his beams above and below, on earth and in heaven; he burnt up the grass in the fields and scorched the faces of princes as well as of poorer folk. But in a short time he began to grow tired of his might, for there seemed nothing left for him to do. Discontent once more filled his soul, and when a cloud covered his face and hid the earth from him, he cried in his anger:

"Does the cloud hold captive my rays, and is it mightier than I? Oh, that I were a cloud, and mightier than any!"

And the mountain spirit answered, "Your wish is heard; a cloud you shall be!"

And a cloud he was, lying between the sun and the earth. It caught the sun's beams and held them, and to his joy the earth grew green again and flowers blossomed. But that was not enough for him, and for days and weeks he poured forth rain till the rivers overflowed their banks, and the crops of rice stood in water.

Towns and villages were destroyed by the power of the rain. Only the great rock on the mountain side remained unmoved. The cloud was amazed at the sight, and cried in wonder:

"Is the rock, then, mightier than I? Oh, if I were only that rock!"

And the mountain spirit answered, "Your wish is heard; that rock you shall be!"

And the rock he was, and gloried in his power. Proudly he stood, and neither the heat of the sun nor the force of the rain could move him. "This is better than all!" he said to himself. But one day he heard a strange noise at his feet, and when he looked down to see what it could be, he saw a stonecutter driving tools into his surface. Even while he looked a trembling feeling ran all through him, and a great block broke off and fell upon the ground. Then he cried in his wrath:

"Is a mere child of earth mightier than a rock? Oh, if I were only a man!"

And the mountain spirit answered, "Your wish is heard. A man once more you shall be!"

And a man he was, and in the sweat of his brow he toiled again at his trade of stonecutting. His bed was hard and his food scanty, but he had learned to be satisfied with it, and did not long to be something or somebody else. And as he never asked for things he had not, or desired to be greater and mightier than other people, he was happy at last, and heard the voice of the mountain spirit no longer.

The Ugly Duckling

Hans Christian Andersen

It was so beautiful out in the country. It was summer. The oats were still green, but the wheat was turning yellow. Down in the meadow the grass had been cut and made into haystacks; and there the storks walked on their long red legs talking Egyptian, because that was the language they had been taught by their mothers. The fields were enclosed by woods, and hidden among them were little lakes and pools. Yes, it certainly was lovely out there in the country!

The old castle, with its deep moat surrounding it, lay bathed in sunshine. Between the heavy walls and the edge of the moat there was a narrow strip of land covered by a whole forest of burdock plants. Their leaves were large and some of the stalks were so tall that a child could stand upright under them and imagine that he was in the middle of the wild and lonely woods. Here a duck had built her nest. While she sat waiting for the eggs to hatch, she felt a little sorry for herself because it was taking so long and hardly anybody came to visit her. The other ducks preferred swimming in the moat to sitting under a dock leaf and gossiping.

Finally the eggs began to crack. "Peep ... Peep," they said one after another. The egg yolks had become alive and were sticking out their heads.

"Quack. Quack." said their mother. "Look around you." And the ducklings did; they glanced at the green world about them, and that was what their mother wanted them to do, for green was good for their eyes.

"How big the world is!" piped the little ones, for they had much more space to move around in now than they had had inside the egg.

"Do you think that this is the whole world?" quacked their mother. "The world is much larger than this. It stretches as far as the minister's wheat fields, though I have not been there. ... Are you all here?" The duck got up and turned around to look at her nest. "Oh no, the biggest egg hasn't hatched yet; and I'm so tired of sitting here I wonder how long it will take?" she wailed, and sat down again.

"What's new?" asked an old duck who had come visiting.

"One of the eggs is taking so long," complained the mother duck. "It won't crack. But take a look at the others. They are the sweetest little ducklings you have ever seen; and every one of them looks exactly like their father. That scoundrel hasn't come to visit me once."

"Let me look at the egg that won't hatch," demanded the old duck. "I am sure that it's a turkey egg! I was fooled that way once. You can't imagine what it's like. Turkeys are afraid of the water. I couldn't get them to go into it. I quacked and I nipped them, but nothing helped. Let me see that egg! ... Yes, it's a turkey egg. Just let it lie there. You go and teach your young ones how to swim, that's my advice."

"I have sat on it so long that I suppose I can sit a little longer, at least until they get the hay in," replied the mother duck. "Suit yourself," said the older duck, and went on.

At last the big egg cracked too. "Peep ... Peep," said the young one, and tumbled out. He was big and very ugly.

The mother duck looked at him. "He's awfully big for his age," she said. "He doesn't look like any of the others. I wonder if he could be a turkey? Well, we shall soon see. Into the water he will go, even if I have to kick him to make him do it."

The next day the weather was gloriously beautiful. The surf shone on the forest of burdock plants. The mother duck took her whole brood to the moat. "Quack ... Quack ... " she ordered.

One after another, the little ducklings plunged into the water. For a moment their heads disappeared, but then they popped up again and the little ones floated like so many corks. Their legs knew what to do without being told. All of the new brood swam very nicely, even the ugly one.

"He is no turkey," mumbled the mother. "See how beautifully he uses his legs and how straight he holds his neck. He is my own child and, when you look closely at him, he's quite handsome. ... Quack! Quack! Follow me and I'll take you to the henyard and introduce you to everyone. But stay close to me, so that no one steps on you, and look out for the cat."

They heard an awful noise when they arrived at the henyard. Two families of ducks had got into a fight over the head of an eel. Neither of them got it, for it was swiped by the cat.

"That is the way of the world," said the mother duck, and licked her bill. She would have liked to have had the eel's head herself "Walk nicely," she admonished them. "And remember to bow to the old duck over there. She has Spanish blood in her veins and is the most aristocratic fowl here. That is why she is so fat and has a red rag tied around one of her legs. That is the highest mark of distinction a duck can be given. It means so much that she will never be done away with; and all the other fowl and the human beings know who she is. Quack! Quack! ... Don't walk, waddle like well-brought-up ducklings. Keep your legs far apart, just as your mother and father have always done. Bow your heads and say, 'Quack'!" And that was what the little ducklings did.

Other ducks gathered about them and said loudly, "What do we want that gang here for? Aren't there enough of us already? Pooh! Look how ugly one of them is! He's the last straw!" And one of the ducks flew over and bit the ugly duckling on the neck.

"Leave him alone!" shouted the mother. "He hasn't done anyone any harm."

"He's big and he doesn't look like everybody else!" replied the duck who had bitten him. "And that's reason enough to beat him."

"Very good-looking children you have," remarked the duck with the red rag around one of her legs. "All of them are beautiful except one. He didn't turn out very well. I wish you could make him over again."

"That's not possible, Your Grace," answered the mother duck. "He may not be handsome, but he has a good character and swims as well as the others, if not a little better. Perhaps he will grow handsomer as he grows older and becomes a bit smaller. He was in the egg too long, and that is why he doesn't have the right shape." She smoothed his neck for a moment and then added, "Besides, he's a drake; and it doesn't matter so much what he looks like. He is strong and I am sure he will be able to take care of himself."

"Well, the others are nice," said the old duck. "Make yourself at home, and if you should find an eel's head, you may bring it to me." And they were "at home."

The poor little duckling, who had been the last to hatch and was so ugly, was bitten and pushed and made fun of both by the hens and by the other ducks. The turkey cock (who had been born with spurs on, and therefore thought he was an emperor) rustled his feathers as if he were a full-rigged ship under sail, and strutted up to the duckling. He gobbled so loudly at him that his own face got all red.

The poor little duckling did not know where to turn. How he grieved over his own ugliness, and how sad he was! The poor creature was mocked and laughed at by the whole henyard.

That was the first day; and each day that followed was worse than the one before. The poor duckling was chased and mistreated by everyone, even his own sisters and brothers, who quacked again and again, "If only the cat would get you, you ugly thing!"

Even his mother said, "I wish you were far away." The other ducks bit him and the hens pecked at him. The little girl who came to feed the fowls kicked him.

At last the duckling ran away. He flew over the tops of the bushes, frightening all the little birds so that they flew up into the air. "They, too, think I am ugly," thought the duckling, and closed his eyes — but he kept on running.

Finally he came to a great swamp where wild ducks lived; and here he stayed for the night, for he was too tired to go any farther.

In the morning he was discovered by the wild ducks. They looked at him and one of them asked, "What kind of bird are you?"

The ugly duckling bowed in all directions, for he was trying to be as polite as he knew how.

"You are ugly," said the wild ducks, "but that is no concern of ours, as long as you don't try to marry into our family."

The poor duckling wasn't thinking of marriage. All he wanted was to be allowed to swim among the reeds and drink a little water when he was thirsty.

He spent two days in the swamp; then two wild geese came—or rather, two wild ganders, for they were males. They had been hatched not long ago; therefore they were both frank and bold.

"Listen, comrade," they said. "You are so ugly that we like you. Do you want to migrate with us? Not far from here there is a marsh where some beautiful wild geese live. They are all lovely maidens, and you are so ugly that you may seek your fortune among them. Come along."

"Bang! Bang!" Two shots were heard and both ganders fell down dead among the reeds, and the water turned red from their blood.

"Bang! Bang!" Again came the sound of shots, and a flock of wild geese flew up.

The whole swamp was surrounded by hunters; from every direction came the awful noise. Some of the hunters had hidden behind bushes or among the reeds but others, screened from sight by the leaves, sat on the long, low branches of the trees that stretched out over the swamp. The blue smoke from the guns lay like a fog over the water and along the trees. Dogs came splashing through the marsh, and they bent and broke the reeds.

The poor little duckling was terrified. He was about to tuck his head under his wing, in order to hide, when he saw a big dog peering at him through the reeds. The dog's tongue hung out of its mouth and its eyes glistened evilly. It bared its teeth. Splash! It turned away without touching the duckling.

"Oh, thank God!" he sighed. "I am so ugly that even the dog doesn't want to bite me."

The little duckling lay as still as he could while the shots whistled through the reeds. Not until the middle of the afternoon did the shooting stop; but the poor little duckling was still so frightened that he waited several hours longer before taking his head out from under his wing. Then he ran as quickly as he could out of the swamp. Across the fields and the meadows he went, but a wind had come up and he found it hard to make his way against it.

Towards evening he came upon a poor little hut. It was so wretchedly crooked that it looked as if it couldn't make up its mind which way to fall and that was why it was still standing. The wind was blowing so hard that the poor little duckling had to sit down in order not to be blown away. Suddenly he noticed that the door was off its hinges, making a crack; and he squeezed himself through it and was inside.

An old woman lived in the hut with her cat and her hen. The cat was called Sonny and could both arch his back and purr. Oh yes, it could also make sparks if you rubbed its fur the wrong way. The hen had very short legs and that was why she was called Cluck Lowlegs. But she was good at laying eggs, and the old woman loved her as if she were her own child.

In the morning the hen and the cat discovered the duckling. The cat meowed and the hen clucked.

"What is going on?" asked the old woman, and looked around. She couldn't see very well, and when she found the duckling she thought it was a fat, full-grown duck. "What a fine catch!" she exclaimed. "Now we shall have duck eggs, unless it's a drake. We'll give it a try."

So the duckling was allowed to stay for three weeks on probation, but he laid no eggs. The cat was the master of the house and the hen the mistress. They always referred to themselves as "we and the world," for they thought that they were half the world — and the better half at that. The duckling thought that he should be allowed to have a different opinion, but the hen did not agree.

"Can you lay eggs?" she demanded.

"No," answered the duckling.

"Then keep your mouth shut."

And the cat asked, "Can you arch your back? Can you purr? Can you make sparks?"

"No."

"Well, in that case, you have no right to have an opinion when sensible people are talking."

The duckling was sitting in a corner and was in a bad mood. Suddenly he recalled how lovely it could be outside in the fresh air when the sun shone: a great longing to be floating in the water came over the duckling, and he could not help talking about it.

"What is the matter with you?" asked the hen as soon as she had heard what he had to say. "You have nothing to do, that's why you get ideas like that. Lay eggs or purr, and such notions will disappear."

"You have no idea how delightful it is to float in the water, and to dive down to the bottom of a lake and get your head wet," said the duckling.

"Yes, that certainly does sound amusing," said the hen. "You must have gone mad. Ask the cat — he is the most intelligent being I know — ask him whether he likes to swim or dive down to the bottom of a lake.

Don't take my word for anything ... . Ask the old woman, who is the cleverest person in the world; ask her whether she likes to float and to get her head all wet."

"You don't understand me!" wailed the duckling.

"And if I don't understand you, who will? I hope you don't think that you are wiser than the cat or the old woman — not to mention myself. Don't give yourself airs! Thank your Creator for all He has done for you. Aren't you sitting in a warm room, where you can hear intelligent conversation that you could learn something from? While you, yourself, do nothing but say a lot of nonsense and aren't the least bit amusing! Believe me, that's the truth, and I am only telling it to you for your own good. That's how you recognize a true friend: it's someone who is willing to tell you the truth, no matter how unpleasant it is. Now get to work: lay some eggs, or learn to purr and arch your back."

"I think I'll go out into the wide world," replied the duckling.

"Go right ahead!" said the hen.

And the duckling left. He found a lake where he could float in the water and dive to the bottom. There were other ducks, but they ignored him because he was so ugly.

Autumn came and the leaves turned yellow and brown, then they fell from the trees. The wind caught them and made them dance. The clouds were heavy with hail and snow. A raven sat on a fence and screeched, "Ach! Ach!" because it was so cold. When just thinking of how cold it was is enough to make one shiver, what a terrible time the duckling must have had.

One evening just as the sun was setting gloriously, a flock of beautiful birds came out from among the rushes. Their feathers were so white that they glistened; and they had long, graceful necks. They were swans. They made a very loud cry, then they spread their powerful wings. They were flying south to a warmer climate, where the lakes were not frozen in the winter. Higher and higher they circled. The ugly duckling turned round and round in the water like a wheel and stretched his neck up toward the sky; he felt a strange longing. He screeched so piercingly that he frightened himself.

Oh, he would never forget those beautiful birds, those happy birds. When they were out of sight the duckling dived down under the water to the bottom of the lake; and when he came up again he was beside himself. He did not know the name of those birds or where they were going, and yet he felt he loved them as he had never loved any other creatures. He did not envy them. It did not even occur to him to wish that he were so handsome himself. He would have been happy if the other ducks had let him stay in the henyard: that poor, ugly bird!

The weather grew colder and colder. The duckling had to swim round and round in the water, to keep just a little space for himself that wasn't frozen. Each night his hole became smaller and smaller. on all sides of him the ice creaked and groaned. The little duckling had to keep his feet constantly in motion so that the last bit of open water wouldn't become ice. At last he was too tired to swim any more. He sat still. The ice closed in around him and he was frozen fast.

Early the next morning a farmer saw him and with his clogs broke the ice to free the duckling. The man put the bird under his arm and took it home to his wife, who brought the duckling back to life.

The children wanted to play with him. But the duckling was afraid that they were going to hurt him, so he flapped his wings and flew right into the milk pail. From there he flew into a big bowl of butter and then into a barrel of flour. What a sight he was!

The farmer's wife yelled and chased him with a poker. The children laughed and almost fell on top of each other, trying to catch him; and how they screamed! Luckily for the duckling, the door was open. He got out of the house and found a hiding place beneath some bushes, in the newly fallen snow; and there he lay so still, as though there was hardly any life left in him.

It would be too horrible to tell of all the hardship and suffering the duckling experienced that long winter. It is enough to know that he did survive. When again the sun shone warmly and the larks began to sing, the duckling was lying among the reeds in the swamp. Spring had come!

He spread out his wings to fly. How strong and powerful they were! Before he knew it, he was far from the swamp and flying above a beautiful garden. The apple trees were blooming and the lilac bushes stretched their flower-covered branches over the water of a winding canal. Everything was so beautiful: so fresh and green. Out of a forest of rushes came three swans. They ruffled their feathers and floated so lightly on the water. The ugly duckling recognized the birds and felt again that strange sadness come over him.

"I shall fly over to them, those royal birds! And they can hack me to death because I, who am so ugly, dare to approach them! What difference does it make? It is better to be killed by them than to be bitten by the other ducks, and pecked by the hens, and kicked by the girl who tends the henyard; or to suffer through the winter."

And he lighted on the water and swam towards the magnificent swans. When they saw him they ruffled their feathers and started to swim in his direction. They were coming to meet him.

"Kill me," whispered the poor creature, and bent his head humbly while he waited for death. But what was that he saw in the water? It was his own reflection; and he was no longer an awkward, clumsy, grey bird, so ungainly and so ugly. He was a swan!

It does not matter that one has been born in the henyard as long as one has lain in a swan's egg.

He was thankful that he had known so much want, and gone through so much suffering, for it made him appreciate his present happiness and the loveliness of everything about him all the more. The swans made a circle around him and caressed him with their beaks.

Some children came out into the garden. They had brought bread with them to feed the swans. The youngest child shouted, "Look, there's a new one!" All the children joyfully clapped their hands, and they ran to tell their parents.

Cake and bread were cast on the water for the swans. Everyone agreed that the new swan was the most beautiful of them all. The older swans bowed towards him.

He felt so shy that he hid his head beneath his wing. He was too happy, but not proud, for a kind heart can never be proud. He thought of the time when he had been mocked and persecuted. And now everyone said that he was the most beautiful of the most beautiful birds. And the lilac bushes stretched their branches right down to the water for him. The sun shone so warm and brightly. He ruffled his feathers and raised his slender neck, while out of the joy in his heart, he thought, "Such happiness I did not dream of when I was the ugly duckling."

The Selfish Giant
Oscar Wilde

Every afternoon, as they were coming from school, the children used to go and play in the Giant's garden. It was a large lovely garden, with soft green grass. Here and there over the grass stood beautiful flowers like stars, and there were twelve peach-trees that in the spring-time broke out into delicate blossoms of pink and pearl, and in the autumn bore rich fruit. The birds sat on the trees and sang so sweetly that the children used to stop their games in order to listen to them. "How happy we are here!" they cried to each other.

One day the Giant came back. He had been to visit his friend the Cornish ogre, and had stayed with him for seven years. After the seven years were over he had said all that he had to say, for his conversation was limited, and he determined to return to his own castle. When he arrived he saw the children playing in the garden.

"What are you doing here?" he cried in a very gruff voice, and the children ran away.

"My own garden is my own garden," said the Giant; "any one can understand that, and I will allow nobody to play in it but myself." So he built a high wall all round it, and put up a notice-board.

"TRESPASSERS WILL BE PROSECUTED"

He was a very selfish Giant.

The poor children had now nowhere to play. They tried to play on the road, but the road was very dusty and full of hard stones, and they did not like it. They used to wander round the high wall when their lessons were over, and talk about the beautiful garden inside. "How happy we were there," they said to each other.

Then the Spring came, and all over the country there were little blos-soms and little birds. Only in the garden of the Selfish Giant it was still winter. The birds did not care to sing in it as there were no children, and the trees forgot to blossom. Once a beautiful flower put its head out from the grass, but when it saw the notice-board it was so sorry for the children that it slipped back into the ground again, and went off to sleep. The only people who were pleased were the Snow and the Frost. "Spring has forgotten this garden, they cried, "so we will live here all the year round." The Snow covered up the grass with her great white cloak, and the Frost painted all the trees silver. Then they invited the North Wind stay with them, and he came. He was wrapped in furs, and he roared all day about the garden, and blew the chimney-pots down.

"This is a delightful spot," he said, "we must ask the Hail on a visit." So the Hail came. Every day for three hours he rattled on the roof of the castle till he broke most of the slates, and then he ran round and round the garden as fast as he could go. He was dressed in grey, and his breath was like ice.

"I cannot understand why the Spring is so late in coming," said the Selfish Giant, as he sat at the window and looked out at his cold white garden; "I hope there will be a change in the weather."

But the Spring never came, nor the Summer. The Autumn gave golden fruit to every garden, but to the Giant's garden she gave none. "He is too selfish," she said. So it was always winter there, and the North Wind and the Hail, and the Frost, and the Snow danced about through the trees.

One morning the Giant was lying awake in bed when he heard some lovely music. It sounded so sweet to his ears that he thought it must be the King's musicians passing by. It was really only a little linnet singing outside his window, but it was so long since he had heard a bird sing in his garden that it seemed to him to be the most beautiful music in the world. Then the Hail stopped dancing over his head, and the North Wind ceased roaring, and a delicious perfume came to him through the open casement. "I believe the Spring has come at last," said the Giant; and he jumped out of bed and looked out.

What did he see?

He saw a most wonderful sight. Through a little hole in the wall the children had crept in, and they were sitting in the branches of the trees. In every tree that he could see there was a little child. And the trees were so glad to have the children back again that they had covered themselves with blossoms, and were waving their arms gently above the children's heads. The birds were flying about and twittering with delight, and the flowers were looking up through the green grass and laughing. It was a lovely scene, only in one corner it was still winter. It was the farthest corner of the garden, and in it was standing a little boy. He was so small that he could not reach up to the branches of the tree, and he was wandering all round it, crying bitterly. The poor tree was still covered with frost and snow, and the North Wind was blowing and roaring above it. "Climb up! little boy," said the Tree, and it bent its branches down as low as it could; but the boy was too tiny.

And the Giant's heart melted as he looked out. "How selfish I have been!" he said: "now I know why the Spring would not come here. I will put that poor little boy on the top of the tree, and then I will knock down the wall, and my garden shall be the children's playground for ever and ever." He was really very sorry for what he had done.

So he crept downstairs and opened the front door quite softly, and went out into the garden. But when the children saw him they were so frightened that they ran away, and the garden became winter again. Only the little boy did not run for his eyes were so full of tears that he did not see the Giant coming. And the Giant stole up behind him and took him gently in his hand, and put him up into the tree. And the tree broke at once into blossom, and the birds came and sang on it, and the little boy stretched out his two arms and flung them round the Giant's neck, and kissed him. And the other children when they saw that the Giant was not wicked any longer, came running back, and with them came the Spring. "It is your garden now, little children," said the Giant, and he took a great axe and knocked down the wall. And when the people were going to market at twelve o'clock they found the Giant playing with the children in the most beautiful garden they had ever seen.

All day long they played, and in the evening they came to the Giant to bid him good-bye.

"But where is your little companion?" he said: "the boy I put into the tree." The Giant loved him the best because he had kissed him.

"We don't know," answered the children. "He has gone away."

"You must tell him to be sure and come tomorrow," said the Giant. But the children said that they did not know where he lived and had never seen him before; and the Giant felt very sad.

Every afternoon, when school was over, the children came and played with the Giant. But the little boy whom the Giant loved was never seen again. The Giant was very kind to all the children, yet he longed for his first little friend, and often spoke of him. "How I would like to see him!" he used to say.

Years went over, and the Giant grew very old and feeble. He could not play about any more, so he sat in a huge armchair, and watched the children at their games; and admired his garden. "I have many beautiful flowers," he said; "but the children are the most beautiful flowers of all."

One winter morning he looked out of his window as he was dressing. He did not hate the Winter now, for he knew that it was merely the Spring asleep, and that the flowers were resting. Suddenly he rubbed his eyes in wonder and looked and looked. It certainly was a marvelous sight. In the farthest corner of the garden was a tree quite covered with lovely white blossoms. Its branches were golden, and silver fruit hung down from them, and underneath it stood the little boy he had loved.

Downstairs ran the Giant in great joy, and out into the garden. He hastened across the grass, and came near to the child. And when he came quite close his face grew red with anger, and he said, "Who hath dared to wound thee?" For on the palms of the child's hands were the prints of two nails, and the prints of two nails were on the little feet.

"Who hath dared to wound thee?" cried the Giant, "tell me, that I may take my big sword and slay him."

"Nay," answered the child: "but these are the wounds of Love."

"Who art thou?" said the Giant, and a strange awe fell on him, and he knelt before the little child.

And the child smiled on the Giant, and said to him, "You let me play once in your garden, today you shall come with me to my garden, which is Paradise."

And when the children ran in that afternoon, they found the Giant lying dead under the tree, all covered with white blossoms.

The Wonderful Tar-Baby Story
Joel Chandler Harris

"Didn't the fox never catch the rabbit, Uncle Remus?" asked the little boy the next evening.

"He come mighty nigh it, honey, sho's you born — Brer Fox did. One day after Brer Rabbit fool 'im wid dat calamus root, Brer Fox went ter wuk en got 'im some tar, en mix it wid some turkentime, en fix up a contrapshun wat he call a Tar-Baby, en he tuck dish yer Tar-Baby en he sot 'er in de big road, en den he lay off in de bushes fer to see what de news wuz gwineter be. En he didn't hatter wait long, nudder, kaze bimeby here come Brer Rabbit pacin' down de road — lippity-clippity, clippity-lippity — dez ez sassy ez a jay-bird. Brer Fox, he lay low. Brer Rabbit come prancin' 'long twel he spy de Tar-Baby, en den he fotch up on his behime legs like he wus 'stonished. De Tar-Baby, she sot dar, she did, en Brer Fox, he lay low.

" 'Mawnin'!' sez Brer Rabbit, sezee — 'nice wedder dis mawnin',' sezee.

"Tar-Baby ain't sayin' nothin', en Brer Fox, he lay low.

" 'How duz yo' sym'tums seem ter segashuate?' sez Brer Rabbit, sezee.

"Brer Fox, he wink his eye slow, en lay low, en de Tar-Baby, she ain't sayin' nothin'.

" 'How you come on, den? Is you deaf?' sez Brer Rabbit, sezee. 'Kaze if you is, I kin holler louder' sezee.

"Tar-Baby stay still, en Brer Fox, he lay low.

" 'Youer stuck up, dat's w'at you is,' says Brer Rabbit, sezee, 'en I'm gwineter kyore you, dat's w'at I'm a gwineter do,' sezee.

"Brer Fox, he sorter chuckle in his stummick, he did, but Tar-Baby ain't sayin' nothing.

" 'I'm gwineter larn you howter talk ter 'specttubble fokes ef hit's de las' ack,' sez Brer Rabbit, sezee. 'Ef you don't take off dat hat en tell me howdy, I'm gwineter bus' you wide open,' sezee.

"Tar-Baby stay still, en Brer Fox, he lay low.

"Brer Rabbit keep on axin' 'im, en de Tar-Baby, she keep on sayin' nothin', twel present'y Brer Rabbit draw back wid his fis', he did, en blip he tuck 'er side er de head. Right dar's whar he broke his merlasses jug. His fis' stuck, en he can't pull loose. De tar hilt 'im. But Tar-Baby, she stay still, en Brer Fox, he lay low.

" 'Ef you don't lemme loose, I'll knock you agin', sez Brer Rabbit, sezee, en wid dat he fotch 'er a wipe wid de udder han', en dat stuck. Tar-Baby, she ain't sayin' nothin', en Brer Fox, he lay low.

" 'Tu'n me loose, fo' I kick de natal stuffin' outen you,' sez Brer Rabbit, sezee, but de Tar-Baby, she ain't sayin' nothin'. She des hilt on, en den Brer Rabbit lose de use er his feet in de same way. Brer Fox, he lay low. Den Brer Rabbit squall out dat ef de Tars Baby don't tu'n 'im loose he butt 'er cranksided. En den he butted, en his head got stuck. Den Brer Fox, he sa'ntered fort', lookin' des ez innercent ez one er yo' mammy's mockin'-birds.

" 'Howdy, Brer Rabbit,' sez Brer Fox, sezee. 'You look sorter stuck up dis mawnin',' sezee, en den he rolled on de ground en laughed en laughed twel he couldn't laugh no mo'. 'I speck you'll take dinner wid me dis time, Brer Rabbit. I done laid in some calamus root, en I ain't gwineter take no skuse,' sez Brer Fox, sezee."

Here Uncle Remus paused, and drew a two-pound yam out of the ashes. "Did the fox eat the rabbit?" asked the little boy to whom the story had been told.

"Dat's all de fur de tale goes," replied the old man. "He mout, en den again he moutent. Some say Jedge B'ar come long en loosed 'im— some say he didn't. I hear Miss Sally callin'. You better run 'long."

How Mr. Rabbit Was Too Sharp For Mr. Fox

Joel Chandler Harris

"Uncle Remus," said the little boy one evening, when he had found the old man with little or nothing to do, "did the fox kill and eat the rabbit when he caught him with the Tar-Baby?"

"Law, honey, ain't I tell you 'bout dat?" replied the old black man, chuckling slyly. "I 'clar ter grashus I ought er tole you dat, but old man Nod wuz ridin' on my eyeleds 'twel a leetle mo'n I'd a dis'member'd my own name, en den on to dat here come yo' mammy hollerin' atter you.

"W'at I tell you w'en I fus' begin? I tole you Brer Rabbit wuz a monstus soon creetur; leas'ways dat's w'at I laid out fer ter tell you. Well, den, honey, don't you go en make no udder calkalashuns, kaze in dem days Brer Rabbit en his fambly wuz at de head er de gang w'en enny racket wuz on han', en dar dey stayed. 'Fo' you begins fer ter wipe yo' eyes 'bout Brer Rabbit, you wait en see whar'bouts Brer Rabbit gwineter fetch up at. But dat's needer yer ner dar.

"W'en Brer Fox fine Brer Rabbit mixt up wid de Tar-Baby, he feel mighty good, en he roll on de groun' en laff. Bimeby he up'n say, sezee:

" 'Well, I speck I got you dis time, Brer Rabbit,' sezee; 'maybe I ain't, but I speck I is. You been runnin' roun' here sassin' atter me a mighty long time, but I speck you done come ter de een' er de row. You bin cuttin' up yo' capers en bouncin' 'roun' in dis neighberhood ontwel you come ter b'leeve yo'se'f de boss er de whole gang. En den youer allers some'rs whar you got no bizness,' sez Brer Fox, sezee. 'Who ax you fer ter come en strike up a 'quaintance wid dish yer Tar-Baby? En who stuck you up dar whar you iz? Nobody in de roun' worril. You des tuck en jam yo'se'f on dat Tar-Baby widout waitin' fer enny invite,' sez Brer Fox, sezee, 'en dar you is, en dar you'll stay twel I fixes up a bresh-pile and fires her up, kaze I'm gwineter bobby-cue you dis day, sho,' sez Brer Fox, sezee.

"Den Brer Rabbit talk mighty 'umble.

" 'I don't keer w'at you do wid me, Brer Fox,' sezee, 'so you don't fling me in dat brier-patch. Roas' me, Brer Fox,' sezee, 'but don't fling me in dat brierpatch,' sezee.

" 'Hit's so much trouble fer ter kindle a fier,' sez Brer Fox, sezee, 'dat I speck I'll hatter hang you,' sezee.

" 'Hang me des ez high as you please, Brer Fox,' sez Brer Rabbit, sezee, 'but do fer de Lord's sake don't fling me in dat brier-patch,' sezee.

"'I ain't got no string,' sez Brer Fox, sezee, 'en now I speck I'll hatter drown you,' sezee.

"'Drown me des ez deep ez you please, Brer Fox,' sez Brer Rabbit, sezee, 'but do don't fling me in dat brier-patch,' sezee.

"'Dey ain't no water nigh,' sez Brer Fox, sezee, 'en now I speck I'll hatter skin you,' sezee.

"'Skin me, Brer Fox,' sez Brer Rabbit, sezee, 'snatch out my eyeballs, t'ar out my years by de roots, en cut off my legs,' sezee, 'but do please, Brer Fox, don't fing me in dat brier-patch,' sezee.

"Co'se Brer Fox wanter hurt Brer Rabbit bad ez he kin, so he cotch 'im by de behime legs en slung 'im right in de middle er de brier-patch. Dar wuz a considerbul flutter whar Brer Rabbit struck de bushes, en Brer Fox sorter hang 'roun' fer ter see w'at wuz gwineter happen. Bimeby he hear somebody call 'im, en way up de hill he see Brer Rabbit settin' crosslegged on a chinkapin log koamin' de pitch outen his har wid a chip. Den Brer Fox know dat he bin swop off mighty bad. Brer Rabbit wuz bleedzed fer ter fling back some er his sass, en he holler out:

"'Bred en bawn in a brier-patch, Brer Fox—bred en bawn in a brier-patch!' en wid dat he skip out des ez lively ez a cricket in de embers."

Mr. Rabbit and Mr. Bear
Joel Chandler Harris

"Dar wuz one season," said Uncle Remus, pulling thoughtfully at his whiskers, "w'en Brer Fox say to hisse'f dat he speck he better whirl in en plant a goober-patch, en in dem days, mon, hit wuz tech en go. De wud wern't mo'n out'n his mouf 'fo' de groun' 'uz brok'd up en de goobers 'uz planted. Ole Brer Rabbit, he sot off en watch de motions, he did, en he sorter shet one eye en sing to his chilluns:

> " 'Ti-yi! Tungalee!
> I eat um pea, I pick um pea.
> Hit grow in de groun', hit grow so free;
> Ti-yi! dem goober pea.'

"Sho' 'nuff w'en de goobers 'gun ter ripen up, eve'y time Brer Fox go down ter his patch, he fine whar somebody bin grabblin' 'mongst de vines, en he git mighty mad. He sorter speck who de somebody is, but ole Brer Rabbit he cover his tracks so cute dat Brer Fox dunner how ter ketch 'im. Bimeby, one day Brer Fox take a walk all roun' de groun'-pea patch, en 'twan't long 'fo' he fine a crack in de fence whar de rail done bin rub right smoove, en right dar he got'im a trap. He tuck'n ben' down a hick'ry saplin', growin' in de fence-cornder, en tie one een' un a plow-line on de top, en in de udder een' he fix a loop-knot, en dat he fasten wid a trigger right in de crack. Nex' mawnin' w'en ole Brer Rabbit come slippin' long en crope thoo de crack, de loop-knot kotch 'im behime de fo' legs, en de saplin' flew'd up, en dar he wuz 'twix' de heavens en de yeth. Dar he swung, en he fear'd he gwineter fall, en he fear'd he wer'n't gwineter fall. W'ile he wuz a fixin' up a tale fer Brer Fox, he hear a lumberin' down de road, en present'y yer cum ole Brer B'ar amblin' 'long fum whar he bin takin' a bee-tree. Brer Rabbit, he hail 'im:
" 'Howdy, Brer B'ar!'
"Brer Ba'r, he look 'roun en bimeby he see Brer Rabbit swingin' fum de saplin', en he holler out:
" 'Heyo, Brer Rabbit! How you come on dis mawnin'?'
" 'Much oblije, I'm middlin', Brer B'ar,' sez Brer Rabbit, sezee.
"Den Brer B'ar, he ax Brer Rabbit w'at he doin' up dar in de elements, en Brer Rabbit, he up'n say he makin' dollar minnit. Brer B'ar, he say how. Brer Rabbit say he keepin' crows out'n Brer Fox's groun'pea patch, en den he ax Brer B'ar ef he don't wanter make dollar minnit, kaze he

got big fambly er chilluns fer to take keer un, en den he make sech nice skeercrow. Brer B'ar 'low dat he take de job, en den Brer Rabbit show 'im how ter ben' down de saplin', en 'twan't long 'fo' Brer B'ar wuz swingin' up dar in Brer Rabbit place. Den Brer Rabbit, he put out fer Brer Fox house, en w'en he got dar he sing out:

"'Brer Fox! Oh, Brer Fox! Come out yer, Brer Fox, en I'll show you de man w'at bin stealin' yo' goobers.'

"Brer Fox, he grab up his walkin'-stick, en bofe un um went runnin' back down ter der goober-patch, en w'en dey got dar, sho 'nuff, dar wuz ole Brer B'ar.

"'Oh, yes! youer kotch, is you?' sez Brer Fox, en 'fo' Brer B'ar could 'splain, Brer Rabbit he jump up en down, en holler out:

"'Hit 'im in de mouf, Brer Fox; hit 'im in de mouf'; en Brer Fox, he draw back wid de walkin'cane, en blip he tuck 'im, en eve'y time Brer B'ar'd try ter 'splain, Brer Fox'd shower down on him.

"W'iles all dis 'uz gwine on, Brer Rabbit, he slip off en git in a mud-hole en des lef' his eyes stickin' out, kaze he know'd dat Brer B'ar'd be a comin' atter 'im. Sho 'nuff, bimeby here come Brer B'ar down de road, en w'en he git ter de mud-hole, he say:

"'Howdy, Brer Frog; is you seed Brer Rabbit go by yer?'

"'He des gone by,' sez Brer Rabbit, en ole man B'ar tuck off down de road like a skeer'd mule, en Brer Rabbit, he come out en dry hisse'f in de sun, en go home ter his fambly same ez enny udder man."

"The Bear didn't catch the Rabbit, then?" inquired the little boy, sleepily.

"Jump up fum dar, honey!" exclaimed Uncle Remus, by way of reply. "I ain't got no time fer ter be settin' yer proppin' yo' eyeleds open."

The Flood
Marius Barbeau

In the spring of the year, a storm once blew over the face of the earth. It flattened the lodges of the people along the Arctic seacoast. Taking flight, the Innuit crowded into their skin boats and, for greater safety, tied them together with sinew. Soon the water rose out of the sea, surged forth, and covered the flat face of the earth, covered its ruins everywhere from sunrise to sunset.

Dumb with terror the Innuit drifted helplessly for a long time, as the earth sank farther and farther below the waters. A mighty gale swept the waves over the timbered hills, and the uprooted trees began to float around like dead giants. The people broke into lament after the sea had swallowed everything in sight, even the highest mountains.

Night came over the waters and with it bitter cold. Huddled close together in their skin boats, the people shivered and wept. Frostbitten and famished, they slowly succumbed to death. Many of them fell into the dark sea.

By daybreak the wind had fallen, the sea had calmed down. The heat returned. Soon it grew so intense that the garments of the people dried up and the waters fell to a lower level. As the heat of the sun increased, it fell like a sheet of flame upon the survivors exposed in their skin boats. Many were the people who perished on the steaming waters of the Flood.

Now there was a sorcerer, whose name was Son-of-the-Owl. He whipped the sea with his bow and cried out:

"Enough, enough! We have suffered enough!"

And casting his earrings into the deep, he repeated, "Enough! we have suffered enough!" The waters simmered down under the blows of his whip. They ran off the mountains and the hillsides, into the rivers, and down into the sea. And the sea was as we know it.

(From Petitot's record of the Flood, as given him by the Eskimos of the MacKenzie River delta)

Yehl

Marius Barbeau

Yehl—Raven, in the beginning, was like a god; he called things forth out of nothing, and many, many of them came to be.

After Raven had lived on Mospay Island, filling it with life, he moved away to Rosepoint. There he wandered along the sand beach stretching out of sight and felt lonely. He was alone. Then he heard something at his feet and stooped forward, listening.

A small voice was coming out of a clam shell half buried in the fine sand; the shell had just begun to open.

"Whah!" called the Raven in a whisper. "Whah! Come out!" A tiny human face appeared in the center of the shell and stretched its neck to look up at Raven. Then, out of fear, it withdrew between the edges of the opening shell.

Another voice came out of the clam and Raven listened. "Whah! Come out!" whispered he, motioning helpfully with his foot. And a second little human face burst forth, wonder in its eyes, then half withdrew to shelter.

Voices kept coming out of the clam, and Raven called them forth one by one, until a row of human faces, some with eyes still closed, others gazing, with hands spread out, with legs over their heads, still others smiling as people do when they are satisfied.

Raven, no longer lonely, looked on, well pleased with his new deed. He had brought to life the first people in the world.

(Told, in 1939, by Ot'iwans, Big-Eagle—whose surname is Captain Andrew Brown—of the Haida tribe of Massett)

Raven Steals the Moon
Marius Barbeau

One day Raven learned that the old fisherman living alone with his daughter, at North Island, kept hidden in his lodge by the sea a ball of bright light called the moon. And he craved its possession.

In the season when salal berries ripen, he changed himself into a salal leaf and was picked up and swallowed by the fisherman's daughter while she stood in a wild fruit patch. From this leaf, in time, he was born to her as a child, a son whose complexion was dark, and whose nose was long like a bill.

As soon as the child could crawl around the lodge, he began to cry for the moon in the box: "Konk, konk! Moon, moon!" At first the fisherman paid no attention to his whimpering; then he grew tired of it and said to his daughter:

"Give my grandson the ball of light!"

The young mother opened the box, a large wooden box in the corner of the lodge. In this box was another, which she also opened. She found a third box, a little smaller, inside; after the third, a fourth, a fifth ... until she reached the tenth. This last was wrapped up in a network of nettle mesh, which she loosened, to throw the lid off. A flood of light filled the lodge, and the moon appeared inside, bright and round like a ball.

"Take it!" said the young mother to her son, throwing it to him with a deft hand. The child caught it in its first flight through the air, and he was happy with it.

But he soon began to whimper again, and his whimpering turned to tears and sobs. His grandfather, who could not bear to hear him, asked his daughter:

"What ails my grandson?"

The mother explained that the child had still another wish. The roof board over the smoke hole of the lodge had closed out the long, moonless night. This roof board the child now wanted removed.

"Throw the smoke hole open for my grandson!"

No sooner had she thrown the smoke hole open to the sky dotted with stars, than the child changed himself into a bird—the Raven. With the moon in its bill—some say, under one of its wings-the Raven flew up to the smoke hole, where he paused for a moment. The moment after he threw the moon upwards into the sky vault, where it has remained to this day.

(*From a narrative recorded in 1939; narrator: Captain Andrew Brown, a Haida of the Queen Charlotte Islands*)

Rikki-Tikki-Tavi
Rudyard Kipling

At the hole where he went in
Red-Eye called to WrinkleSkin
Hear what little Red-Eye saith: —
'Nag, come up and dance with death!'
Eye to eye and head to head
(Keep the measure, Nag).
This shall end when one is dead
(At thy pleasure, Nag).
Turn for turn and twist for twist
(Run and hide thee, Nag).
Hah! The hooded Death has missed!
(Woe betide thee, Nag!)

This is the story of the great war that Rikki-tikki-tavi fought single-handed, through the bath-rooms of the big bungalow in Segowlee cantonment. Darzee, the tailor-bird, helped him, and Chuchundra, the musk-rat, who never comes out into the middle of the floor, but always creeps round by the wall, gave him advice; but Rikki-tikki did the real fighting.

He was a mongoose, rather like a little cat in his fur and his tail, but quite like a weasel in his head and his habits. His eyes and the end of his restless nose were pink; he could scratch himself anywhere he pleased with any leg, front or back, that he chose to use; he could fluff up his tail till it looked like a bottle-brush, and his war-cry as he scuttled through the long grass was: Rikk-tikk-tikki-tikki-tchk!

One day, a high summer flood washed him out of the burrow where he lived with his father and mother, and carried him, kicking and clucking, down a roadside ditch. He found a little wisp of grass floating there, and clung to it till he lost his senses. When he revived, he was lying in the hot sun on the middle of a garden path, very draggled indeed, and a small boy was saying: 'Here's a dead mongoose. Let's have a funeral.'

'No,' said his mother; 'let's take him in and dry him. Perhaps he isn't really dead.' They took him into the house, and a big man picked him up between his finger and thumb and said he was not dead but half choked; so they wrapped him in cotton-wool, and warmed him over a little fire, and he opened his eyes and sneezed.

'Now,' said the big man (he was an Englishman who had just moved into the bungalow); 'don't frighten him, and we'll see what he'll do.'

It is the hardest thing in the world to frighten a mongoose, because he is eaten up from nose to tail with curiosity. The motto of all the mongoose family is, 'Run and find out'; and Rikki-tikki was a true mongoose. He looked at the cotton-wool, decided that it was not good to eat, ran all round the table, sat up and put his fur in order, scratched himself, and jumped on the small boy's shoulder.

'Don't be frightened, Teddy,' said his father. 'That's his way of making friends.'

'Ouch! He's tickling under my chin,' said Teddy.

Rikki-tikki looked down between the boy's collar and neck, snuffed at his ear, and climbed down to the floor, where he sat rubbing his nose.

'Good gracious,' said Teddy's mother, 'and that's a wild creature! I suppose he's so tame because we've been kind to him.'

'All mongooses are like that,' said her husband. 'If Teddy doesn't pick him up by the tail, or try to put him in a cage, he'll run in and out of the house all day long. Let's give him something to eat.'

They gave him a little piece of raw meat. Rikki-tikki liked it immensely, and when it was finished he went out into the veranda and sat in the sunshine and fluffed up his fur to make it dry to the roots. Then he felt better.

'There are more things to find out about in this house, he said to himself, 'than all my family could find out in all their lives. I shall certainly stay and find out.'

He spent all that day roaming over the house. He nearly drowned himself in the bath-tubs; put his nose into the ink on a writing-table, and burnt it on the end of the big man's cigar, for he climbed up in the big man's lap to see how writing was done. At nightfall he ran into Teddy's nursery to watch how kerosene lamps were lighted, and when Teddy went to bed Rikki-tikki climbed up too; but he was a restless companion, because he had to get up and attend to every noise all through the night, and find out what made it. Teddy's mother and father came in, the last thing, to look at their boy, and Rikki-tikki was awake on the pillow. 'I don't like that,' said Teddy's mother; 'he may bite the child.' 'He'll do no such thing,' said the father. 'Teddy's safer with that little beast than if he had a bloodhound to watch him. If a snake came into the nursery now.'

But Teddy's mother wouldn't think of anything so awful.

Early in the morning Rikki-tikki came to early breakfast in the veranda riding on Teddy's shoulder, and they gave him banana and some boiled egg; and he sat on all their laps one after the other, because every well-brought-up mongoose always hopes to be a house-mongoose some day and have rooms to run about in; and Rikki-tikki's mother (she used to live in the General's house at Segowlee) had carefully told Rikki what to do if ever he came across white men.

Then Rikki-tikki went out into the garden to see what was to be seen. It was a large garden, only half cultivated, with bushes, as big as summer-houses, of Marshal Niel roses; lime and orange trees, clumps of bamboos, and thickets of high grass. Rikki-tikki licked his lips. 'This is a splendid hunting-ground,' he said, and his tail grew bottle-brushy at the thought of it, and he scuttled up and down the garden, snuffing here and there till he heard very sorrowful voices in a thorn-bush. It was Darzee, the tailor-bird, and his wife. They had made a beautiful nest by pulling two big leaves together and stitching them up the edges with fibres, and had filled the hollow with cotton and downy fluff. The nest swayed to and fro, as they sat on the rim and cried.

'What is the matter?' asked Rikki-tikki.

'We are very miserable,' said Darzee. 'One of our babies fell out of the nest yesterday and Nag ate him.'

'H'm!' said Rikkitikki, 'that is very sad — but I am a stranger here. Who is Nag?'

Darzee and his wife only cowered down in the nest without answering, for from the thick grass at the foot of the bush there came a low hiss — a horrid cold sound that made Rikki-tikki jump back two clear feet. Then inch by inch out of the grass rose up the head and spread hood of Nag, the big black cobra, and he was five feet long from tongue to tail. When he had lifted one-third of himself clear of the ground, he stayed balancing to and fro exactly as a dandelion-tuft balances in the wind, and he looked at Rikki-tikki with the wicked snake's eyes that never change their expression, whatever the snake may be thinking of.

'Who is Nag?' said he. 'I am Nag. The great God Brahm put his mark upon all our people, when the first cobra spread his hood to keep the sun off Brahm as he slept. Look, and be afraid!'

He spread out his hood more than ever, and Rikki-tikki saw the spectacle-mark, on the back of it that looks exactly like the eye part of a hook-and-eye fastening. He was afraid for the minute; but it is impossible for a mongoose to stay frightened for any length of time, and though Rikki-tikki had never met a live cobra before, his mother had fed him on dead ones, and he knew that all a grown mongoose's business in life was to fight and eat snakes. Nag knew that too and, at the bottom of his cold heart, he was afraid.

'Well,' said Rikki-tikki, and his tail began to fluff up again, 'marks or no marks, do you think it is right for you to eat fledgelings out of a nest?'

Nag was thinking to himself, and watching the least little movement in the grass behind Rikki-tikki. He knew that mongooses in the garden meant death sooner or later for him and his family; but he wanted to get

Rikki-tikki off his guard. So he dropped his head a little, and put it on one side.

'Let us talk,' he said. 'You eat eggs. Why should not I eat birds?'

'Behind you! Look behind you!' sang Darzee.

Rikki-tikki knew better than to waste time in staring. He jumped up in the air as high as he could go, and just under him whizzed by the head of Nagaina, Nag's wicked wife. She had crept up behind him as he was talking, to make an end of him; and he heard her savage hiss as the stroke missed. He came down almost across her back, and if he had been an old mongoose he would have known that then was the time to break her back with one bite; but he was afraid of the terrible lashing return-stroke of the cobra. He bit, indeed, but did not bite long enough, and he jumped clear of the whisking tail, leaving Nagaina torn and angry.

'Wicked, wicked Darzee!' said Nag, lashing up as high as he could reach toward the nest in the thorn-bush; but Darzee had built it out of reach of snakes, and it only swayed to and fro.

Rikki-tikki felt his eyes growing red and hot (when a mongoose's eyes grow red, he is angry), and he sat back on his tail and hind legs like a little kangaroo, and looked all round him, and chattered with rage. But Nag and Nagaina had disappeared into the grass. When a snake misses its stroke, it never says anything or gives any sign of what it means to do next. Rikki-tikki did not care to follow them, for he did not feel sure that he could manage two snakes at once. So he trotted off to the gravel path near the house, and sat down to think. It was a serious matter for him. If you read the old books of natural history, you will find they say that when the mongoose fights the snake and happens to get bitten, he runs off and eats some herb that cures him. That is not true. The victory is only a matter of quickness of eye and quickness of foot, — snake's blow against mongoose's jump, — and as no eye can follow the motion of a snake's head when it strikes, this makes things much more wonderful than any magic herb. Rikki-tikki knew he was a young mongoose, and it made him all the more pleased to think that he had managed to escape a blow from behind. It gave him confidence in himself, and when Teddy came running down the path, Rikki-tikki was ready to be petted. But just as Teddy was stooping, something wriggled a little in the dust, and a tiny voice said: 'Be careful. I am Death?' It was Karait, the dusty brown snakeling that lies for choice on the dusty earth; and his bite is as dangerous as the cobra's. But he is so small that nobody thinks of him, and so he does the more harm to people.

Rikki-tikki's eyes grew red again, and he danced up to Karait with the peculiar rocking, swaying motion that he had inherited from his family. It looks very funny, but it is so perfectly balanced a gait that you can fly off from it at any angle you please; and in dealing with snakes this is an advantage. If Rikki-tikki had only known, he was doing a much more dangerous thing than fighting Nag, for Karait is so small, and can turn so quickly, that unless Rikki bit him close to the back of the head, he would get the return-stroke in his eye or his lip. But Rikki did not know: his eyes were all red, and he rocked back and forth, looking for a good place to hold. Karait struck out, Rikki jumped sideways and tried to run in, but the wicked little dusty gray head lashed within a fraction of his shoulder, and he had to jump over the body, and the head followed his heels close.

Teddy shouted to the house: 'Oh, look here! Our mongoose is killing a snake;' and Rikki-tikki heard a scream from Teddy's mother. His father ran out with a stick, but by the time he came up, Karait had lunged out once too far, and Rikki-tikki had sprung, jumped on the snake's back, dropped his head far between his fore-legs, bitten as high up the back as he could get hold, and rolled away. That bite paralysed Karait, and Rikki-tikki was just going to eat him up from the tail, after the custom of his family at dinner, when he remembered that a full meal makes a slow mongoose, and if he wanted all his strength and quickness ready, he must keep himself thin. He went away for a dust-bath under the castor-oil bushes, while Teddy's father beat the dead Karait. 'What is the use of that?' thought Rikkitikki; 'I have settled it all;' and then Teddy's mother picked him up from the dust and hugged him, crying that he had saved Teddy from death, and Teddy's father said that he was a providence, and Teddy looked on with big scared eyes. RikkiTikki was rather amused at all the fuss, which, of course, he did not understand. Teddy's mother might just as well have petted Teddy for playing in the dust. Rikki was thoroughly enjoying himself.

That night at dinner, walking to and fro among the wine-glasses on the table, he might have stuffed himself three times over with nice things; but he remembered Nag and Nagaina, and though it was very pleasant to be patted and petted by Teddy's mother, and to sit on Teddy's shoulder, his eyes would get red from time to time, and he would go off into his long war-cry of 'Rikk-tikk-tikki-t-tchk!'

Teddy carried him off to bed, and insisted on Rikki-tikki sleeping under his chin. Rikki-tikki was too well bred to bite or scratch, but as soon as Teddy was asleep he went off for his nightly walk round the house, and in the dark he ran up against Chuchundra, the musk-rat, creeping round by the wall. Chuchundra is a broken-hearted little beast. He whimpers and cheeps all the night, trying to make up his mind to run into the middle of the room; but he never gets there.

'Don't kill me,' said Chuchundra, almost weeping. 'Rikki-tikki, don't kill me!'

'Do you think a snake-killer kills musk rats?' said Rikki-tikki scornfully.

'Those who kill snakes get killed by snakes,' said Chuchundra, more sorrowfully than ever. 'And how am I to be sure that Nag won't mistake me for you some dark night?'

'There's not the least danger,' said Rikki-tikki; 'but Nag is in the garden, and I know you don't go there.'

'My cousin Chua, the rat, told me,' said Chuchundra, and then he stopped.

'Told you what?'

'H'sh! Nag is everywhere, Rikki-tikki. You should have talked to Chua in the garden.'

'I didn't — so you must tell me. Quick, Chuchundra, or I'll bite you!'

Chuchundra sat down and cried till the tears rolled off his whiskers. 'I am a very poor man,' he sobbed. 'I never had spirit enough to run out into the middle of the room. H'sh! I mustn't tell you anything. Can't you hear, Rikki-tikki?'

Rikki-tikki listened. The house was as still as still, but he thought he could just catch the faintest scratch-scratch in the world, — a noise as faint as that of a wasp walking on a window-pane, — the dry scratch of a snake's scales on brickwork.

'That's Nag or Nagaina,' he said to himself; 'and he is crawling into the bath-room sluice. You're right, Chuchundra; I should have talked to Chua.'

He stole off to Teddy's bath-room, but there was nothing there, and then to Teddy's mother's bathroom. At the bottom of the smooth plaster wall there was a brick pulled out to make a sluice for the bath-water, and as Rikki-tikki stole in by the masonry curb where the bath is put, he heard Nag and Nagaina whispering together outside in the moonlight.

'When the house is emptied of people, 'said Nagaina to her husband, 'he will have to go away, and then the garden will be our own again. Go in quietly, and remember that the big man who killed Karait is the first one to bite. Then come out and tell me, and we will hunt for Rikki-tikki together.'

'But are you sure that there is anything to be gained by killing the people?' said Nag.

'Everything. When there were no people in the bungalow, did we have any mongoose in the garden? So long as the bungalow is empty, we are king and queen of the garden; and remember that as soon as our eggs in the melon-bed hatch (as they may tomorrow), our children will need room and quiet.'

'I had not thought of that,' said Nag. 'I will go, but there is no need that we should hunt for Rikki-tikki afterward. I will kill the big man and his wife, and the child if I can, and come away quietly. Then the bungalow will be empty, and Rikki-tikki will go.'

Rikki-tikki tingled all over with rage and hatred at this, and then Nag's head came through the sluice, and his five feet of cold body followed it. Angry as he was, Rikki-tikki was very frightened as he saw the size of the big cobra. Nag coiled himself up, raised his head, and looked into the bathroom in the dark, and Rikki could see his eyes glitter.

'Now, if I kill him here, Nagaina will know; and if I fight him on the open floor, the odds are in his favour. What am I to do?' said Rikki-tikki-tavi.

Nag waved to and fro, and then Rikki-tikki heard him drinking from the biggest waterjar that was used to fill the bath. 'That is good,' said the snake. 'Now, when Karait was killed, the big man had a stick. He may have that stick still, but when he comes in to bathe in the morning he will not have a stick. I shall wait here till he comes. Nagaina-you hear me? — I shall wait here in the cool till daytime.'

There was no answer from outside, so Rikki-tikki knew Nagaina had gone away. Nag coiled himself down, coil by coil, round the bulge at the bottom of the waterjar, and Rikki-tikki stayed still as death. After an hour he began to move, muscle by muscles towards the jar. Nag was asleep, and Rikki-tikki looked at his big back, wondering which would be the best place for a good hold. 'If I don't break his back at the first jump,' said Rikki, 'he can still fight; and if he fights — O Rikki!' He looked at the thickness of the neck below the hood, but that was too much for him; and a bite near the tail would only make Nag savage.

'It must be the head,' he said at last; 'the head above the hood; and, when I am once there, I must not let go.'

Then he jumped. The head was lying a little clear of the waterjar, under the curve of it; and, as his teeth met, Rikki braced his back against the bulge of the red earthenware to hold down the head. This gave him just one second's purchase, and he made the most of it. Then he was battered to and fro as a rat is shaken by a dog — to and fro on the floor, up and down, and round in great circles, but his eyes were red and he held on as the body cartwhipped over the floor, upsetting the tin dipper and the soap-dish and the flesh-brush, and banged against the tin side of the bath. As he held he closed his jaws tighter and tighter, for he made sure he would be banged to death, and, for the honour of his family, he preferred to be found with his teeth locked. He was dizzy, aching, and felt shaken to pieces when something went off like a thunderclap just behind him; a hot wind knocked him senseless and red fire singed his fur. The big man had been wakened by the noise, and had fired both barrels of a shot-gun into Nag just behind the hood.

Rikki-tikki held on with his eyes shut, for now he was quite sure he was dead; but the head did not move, and the big man picked him up and said: 'It's the mongoose again, Alice; the little chap has saved our lives now.' Then Teddy's mother came in with a very white face, and saw what was left of Nag, and Rikki-tikki dragged himself to Teddy's bedroom and spent half the rest of the night shaking himself tenderly to find out whether he really was broken into forty pieces, as he fancied.

When morning came he was very stiff, but well pleased with his doings. 'Now I have Nagaina to settle with, and she will be worse than five Nags, and there's no knowing when the eggs she spoke of will hatch. Goodness! I must go and see Darzee,' he said.

Without waiting for breakfast, Rikki-tikki ran to the thorn-bush where Darzee was singing a song of triumph at the top of his voice. The news of Nag's death was all over the garden, for the sweeper had thrown the body on the rubbish-heap.

'Oh, you stupid tuft of feathers!' said Rikki-tikki angrily. 'Is this the time to sing?'

'Nag is dead — is dead — is dead!' sang Darzee. 'The valiant Rikki-tikki caught him by the head and held fast. The big man brought the bang-stick, and Nag fell in two pieces! He will never eat my babies again.'

'All that's true enough; but where's Nagaina?' said Rikki-tikki, looking carefully round him.

'Nagaina came to the bath-room sluice and called for Nag,' Darzee went on; 'and Nag came out on the end of a stick — the sweeper picked him up on the end of a stick and threw him upon the rubbish-heap. Let us sing about the great, the red-eyed Rikki-tikki!' and Darzee filled his throat and sang.

'If I could get up to your nest, I'd roll your babies out!' said Rikki-tikki. 'You don't know when to do the right thing at the right time. You're safe enough in your nest there, but it's war for me down here. Stop singing a minute, Darzee.'

'For the great, the beautiful Rikki-tikki's sake I will stop,' said Darzee. 'What is it, O Killer of the terrible Nag?'

'Where is Nagaina, for the third time?'

'On the rubbish-heap by the stables, mourning for Nag. Great is Rikki-tikki with the white teeth.'

'Bother my white teeth! Have you ever heard where she keeps her eggs?'

'In the melon-bed, on the end nearest the wall, where the sun strikes nearly all day. She hid them there weeks ago.'

'And you never thought it worth while to tell me? The end nearest the wall, you said?'

'Rikki-tikki, you are not going to eat her eggs?'

'Not eat exactly; no. Darzee, if you have a grain of sense you will fly off to the stables and pretend that your wing is broken, and let Nagaina chase you away to this bush? I must get to the melon-bed, and if I went there now she'd see me.'

Darzee was a feather-brained little fellow who could never hold more than one idea at a time in his head; and just because he knew that Nagaina's children were born in eggs like his own, he didn't think at first that it was fair to kill them. But his wife was a sensible bird, and she knew that cobra's eggs meant young cobras later on; so she flew off from the nest, and left Darzee to keep the babies warm, and continue his song about the death of Nag. Darzee was very like a man in some ways.

She fluttered in front of Nagaina by the rubbishheap, and cried out, 'Oh, my wing is broken! The boy in the house threw a stone at me and broke it.' Then she fluttered more desperately than ever.

Nagaina lifted up her head and hissed, 'You warned Rikki-tikki when I would have killed him. Indeed and truly, you've chosen a bad place to be lame in.' And she moved toward Darzee's wife, slipping along over the dust.

'The boy broke it with a stone!' shrieked Darzee's wife.

'Well! It may be some consolation to you when you're dead to know that I shall settle accounts with the boy. My husband lies on the rubbish-heap this morning, but before night the boy in the house will lie very still. What is the use of running away? I am sure to catch you. Little fool, look at me!'

Darzee's wife knew better than to do that, for a bird who looks at a snake's eyes gets so frightened that she cannot move. Darzee's wife fluttered on, piping sorrowfully, and never leaving the ground, and Nagaina quickened her pace.

Rikki-tikki heard them going up the path from the stables, and he raced for the end of the melon-patch near the wall. There, in the warm litter above the melons, very cunningly hidden, he found twenty-five eggs, about the size of a bantam's eggs, but with whitish skins instead of shells.

'I was not a day too soon,' he said; for he could see the baby cobras curled up inside the skin, and he knew that the minute they were hatched they could each kill a man or a mongoose. He bit off the tops of the eggs as fast as he could, taking care to crush the young cobras, and turned over the litter from time to time to see whether he had missed any. At last there were only three eggs left, and Rikki-tikki began to chuckle to himself, when he heard Darzee's wife screaming:

'Rikki-tikki, I led Nagaina toward the house, and she has gone into the veranda, and—oh, come quickly—she means killing!'

Rikki-tikki smashed two eggs, and tumbled backward down the melon-bed with the third egg in his mouth, and scuttled to the veranda as hard as he could put foot to the ground. Teddy and his mother and father were there at early breakfast; but Rikki-tikki saw that they were not eating anything. They sat stone-still, and their faces were white. Nagaina was coiled up on the matting by Teddy's chair, within easy striking distance of Teddy's bare leg, and she was swaying to and fro, singing a song of triumph.

'Son of the big man that killed Nag,' she hissed, ' stay still. I am not ready yet. Wait a little. Keep very still, all you three! If you move I strike, and if you do not move I strike. Oh, foolish people, who killed my Nag!'

Teddy's eyes were fixed on his father, and all his father could do was to whisper, 'Sit still, Teddy. You mustn't move. Teddy, keep still.'

Then Rikki-tikki came up and cried: 'Turn round, Nagaina; turn and fight!'

'All in good time,' said she, without moving her eyes. 'I will settle my account with you presently. Look at your friends, Rikki-tikki. They are still and white. They are afraid. They dare not move, and if you come a step nearer I strike.'

'Look at your eggs,' said Rikki-tikki, 'in the melon-bed near the wall. Go and look, Nagaina!'

The big snake turned half round, and saw the egg on the veranda. 'Ah-h! Give it to me,' she said.

Rikki tikki put his paws one on each side of the egg, and his eyes were blood-red. 'What price for a snake's egg? For a young cobra? For a young king-cobra? For the last — the very last of the brood? The ants are eating all the others down by the melon-bed.'

Nagaina spun clear round, forgetting everything for the sake of the one egg; and Rikki-tikki saw Teddy's father shoot out a big hand, catch Teddy by the shoulder, and drag him across the little table with the tea-cups, safe and out of reach of Nagaina.

'Tricked! Tricked! Tricked! Rikk-tck-tck!' chuckled Rikki-tikki. 'The boy is safe, and it was I — I — I that caught Nag by the hood last night in the bath-room.' Then he began to jump up and down, all four feet together, his head close to the floor. 'He threw me to and fro, but he could not shake me off. He was dead before the big man blew him in two. I did it! Rikki-tikki-tck-tck! Come then, Nagaina. Come and fight with me. You shall not be a widow long.'

Nagaina saw that she had lost her chance of killing Teddy, and the egg lay between Rikki-tikki's paws. 'Give me the egg, Rikki-tikki. Give me the last of my eggs, and I will go away and never come back,' she said, lowering her hood.

'Yes, you will go away, and you will never come back; for you will go to the rubbish-heap with Nag. Fight, widow! The big man has gone for his gun! Fight!'

Rikki-tikki was bounding all round Nagaina, keeping just out of reach of her stroke, his little eyes like hot coals. Nagaina gathered herself together, and flung out at him. Rikki-tikki jumped up and backwards. Again and again and again she struck, and each time her head came with a whack on the matting of the veranda and she gathered herself together like a watch-spring. Then Rikki-tikki danced in a circle to get behind her, and Nagaina spun round to keep her head to his head, so that the rustle of her tail on the matting sounded like dry leaves blown along by the wind.

He had forgotten the egg. It still lay on the veranda, and Nagaina came nearer and nearer to it, till at last, while Rikkitikki was drawing breath, she caught it in her mouth, turned to the veranda steps, and flew like an arrow down the path, with Rikki-tikki behind her.

When the cobra runs for her life, she goes like a whip-lash flicked across a horse's neck. Rikki-tikki knew that he must catch her, or all the trouble would begin again. She headed straight for the long grass by the thorn-bush, and as he was running Rikki-tikki heard Darzee still singing his foolish little song of triumph. But Darzee's wife was wiser. She flew off her nest as Nagaina came along, and flapped her wings about Nagaina's head. If Darzee had helped they might have turned her; but Nagaina only lowered her hood and went on. Still, the instant's delay brought Rikki-tikki up to her, and as she plunged into the rat-hole where she and Nag used to live, his little white teeth were clenched on her tail, and he went down with her—and very few mongooses, however wise and old they may be, care to follow a cobra into its hole. It was dark in the hole; and Rikki-tikki never knew when it might open out and give Nagaina room to turn and strike at him. He held on savagely, and stuck out his feet to act as brakes on the dark slope of the hot, moist earth. Then the grass by the mouth of the hole stopped waving, and Darzee said: 'It is all over with Rikki-tikki! We must sing his deathsong. Valiant Rikki-tikki is dead! For Nagaina will surely kill him underground.'

So he sang a very mournful song that he made up on the spur of the minute, and just as he got to the most touching part the grass quivered again, and Rikki-tikki, covered with dirt, dragged himself out of the hole leg by leg, licking his whiskers. Darzee stopped with a little shout. Rikki-tikki shook some of the dust out of his fur and sneezed. 'It is all over,' he said. 'The widow will never come out again.' And the red ants that live between the grass stems heard him, and began to troop down one after another to see if he had spoken the truth.

Rikki-tikki curled himself up in the grass and slept where he was— slept and slept till it was late in the afternoon, for he had done a hard day's work.

'Now,' he said, when he awoke, 'I will go back to the house. Tell the Coppersmith, Darzee, and he will tell the garden that Nagaina is dead.'

The Coppersmith is a bird who makes a noise exactly like the beating of a little hammer on a copper pot; and the reason he is always making it is because he is the town-crier to every Indian garden, and tells all the news to everybody who cares to listen. As Rikki-tikki went up the path, he heard his 'attention' notes like a tiny dinner-gong; and then the steady 'Ding-dong-tock! Nag is dead—dong! Nagaina is dead! Ding-dong-tock!' That set all the birds in the garden singing, and the frogs croaking; for Nag and Nagaina used to eat frogs as well as little birds.

When Rikki got to the house, Teddy and Teddy's mother (she looked very white still, for she had been fainting) and Teddy's father came out and almost cried over him; and that night he ate all that was given him till he could eat no more, and went to bed on Teddy's shoulder, where Teddy's mother saw him when she came to look late at night.

'He saved our lives and Teddy's life,' she said to her husband. 'Just think, he saved all our lives.'

Rikki-tikki woke up with a jump, for the mongooses are light sleepers.

'Oh, it's you,' said he. 'What are you bothering for? All the cobras are dead; and if they weren't, I'm here.'

Rikki-tikki had a right to be proud of himself; but he did not grow too proud, and he kept that garden as a mongoose should keep it, with tooth and jump and spring and bite, till never a cobra dared show its head inside the walls.

Redruff

E. Thompson Seton

1

Down the Wooded slope of Taylor's Hill the Mother Partridge led her brood; down toward the crystal brook that by some strange whim was called Mud Creek. Her little ones were one day old but already quick on foot, and she was taking them for the first time to drink.

She walked slowly, crouching low as she went, for the woods were full of enemies. She was uttering a soft little cluck in her throat, a call to the little balls of mottled down that on their tiny pink legs came toddling after, and peeping softly and plaintively if left even a few inches behind, and seeming so fragile they made the very chicadees look big and coarse. There were twelve of them, but Mother Grouse watched them all, and she watched every bush and tree and thicket, and the whole woods and the sky itself. Always for enemies she seemed seeking — friends were too scarce to be looked for — and an enemy she found. Away across the level beaver meadow was a great brute of a fox. He was coming their way, and in a few moments would surely wind them or strike their trail. There was no time to lose.

"Krrr! Krrr!" (Hide! Hide!) cried the mother in a low firm voice, and the little bits of things, scarcely bigger than acorns and but a day old, scattered far (a few inches) apart to hide. One dived under a leaf, another between two roots, a third crawled into a curl of birch-bark, a fourth into a hole, and so on, till all were hidden but one who could find no cover, so squatted on a broad yellow chip and lay very flat, and closed his eyes very tight, sure that now he was safe from being seen. They ceased their frightened peeping and all was still.

Mother Partridge flew straight toward the dreaded beast, alighted fearlessly a few yards to one side of him, and then flung herself on the ground, flopping as though winged and lame — oh, so dreadfully lame — and whining like a distressed puppy. Was she begging for mercy — mercy from a bloodthirsty, cruel fox? Oh, dear no! She was no fool. One often hears of the cunning of the fox. Wait and see what a fool he is compared with a mother-partridge. Elated at the prize so suddenly within his reach, the fox turned with a dash and caught — at least, no, he didn't quite catch the bird; she flopped by chance just a foot out of reach. He followed with another jump and would have seized her this time surely, but somehow a sapling came just between, and the partridge dragged herself awkwardly away and under a log, but the great brute snapped his jaws and bounded over the log, while she, seeming a trifle less lame, made another clumsy forward spring and tumbled down a bank, and Reynard, keenly following, almost caught her tail, but, oddly enough, fast as he went and leaped, she still seemed just a trifle faster. It was most extraordinary. A winged partridge and he, Reynard, the Swift-foot, had not caught her in five minutes' racing. It was really shameful. But the partridge seemed to gain strength as the fox put forth his, and after a quarter of a mile race, racing that was somehow all away from Taylor's Hill, the bird got unaccountably quite well, and, rising with a derisive whirr, flew off through the woods leaving the fox utterly dumfounded to realize that he had been made a fool of, and, worst of all, he now remembered that this was not the first time he had been served this very trick, though he never knew the reason for it.

Meanwhile Mother Partridge skimmed in a great circle and came by a roundabout way back to the little fuzzballs she had left hidden in the woods.

With a wild bird's keen memory for places, she went to the very grass-blade she last trod on, and stood for a moment fondly to admire the perfect stillness of her children. Even at her step not one had stirred, and the little fellow on the chip, not so very badly concealed after all, had not budged nor did he now; he only closed his eyes a tiny little bit harder, till the mother said:

"K-reet!" (Come, children) and instantly like a fairy story, every hole gave up its little baby-partridge, and the wee fellow on the chip, the biggest of them all really, opened his big-little eyes and ran to the shelter of her broad tail, with a sweet little 'peep peep' which an enemy could not have heard three feet away, but which his mother could not have missed thrice as far, and all the other thimblefuls of down joined in, and no doubt thought themselves dreadfully noisy, and were proportionately happy.

The sun was hot now. There was an open space to cross on the road to the water, and, after a careful lookout for enemies, the mother gathered the little things under the shadow of her spread fantail and kept off all danger of sunstroke until they reached the brier thicket by the stream.

Here a cottontail rabbit leaped out and gave them a great scare. But the flag of truce he carried behind was enough. He was an old friend; and among other things the little ones learned that day that Bunny always sails under a flag of truce, and lives up to it too.

And then came the drink, the purest of living water, though silly men had called it Mud Creek.

At first the little fellows didn't know how to drink, but they copied their mother, and soon learned to drink like her and give thanks after every sip. There they stood in a row along the edge, twelve little brown and golden balls on twenty-four little pinktoed, in-turned feet, with twelve sweet little golden heads gravely bowing, drinking and giving thanks like their mother.

Then she led them by short stages, keeping the cover, to the far side of the beaver-meadow, where was a great grassy dome. The mother had made a note of this dome some time before. It takes a number of such domes to raise a brood of partridges. For this was an ant's nest. The old one stepped on top, looked about a moment, then gave half a dozen vigorous rakes with her claws. The friable ant-hill was broken open, and the earthen galleries scattered in ruins down the slope. The ants swarmed out and quarrelled with each other for lack of a better plan. Some ran around the hill with vast energy and little purpose, while a few of the more sensible began to carry away fat white eggs. But the old partridge, coming to the little ones, picked up one of these juicy-looking bags and clucked and dropped it, and picked it up again and again and clucked, then swallowed it. The young ones stood around, then one little yellow fellow, the one that sat on the chip, picked up an ant-egg, dropped it a few times, then yielding to a sudden impulse, swallowed it, and so had learned to eat. Within twenty minutes even the runt had learned, and a merry time they had scrambling after the delicious eggs as their mother broke open more ant-galleries, and sent them and their contents rolling down the bank, till every little partridge had so crammed his little crop that he was positively misshapen and could eat no more.

Then all went cautiously up the stream, and on a sandy bank, well screened by brambles, they lay for all that afternoon, and learned how pleasant it was to feel the cool powdery dust running between their hot little toes. With their strong bent for copying, they lay on their sides like their mother and scratched with their tiny feet and flopped with their wings, though they had no wings to flop with, only a little tag among the down on each side, to show where the wings would come. That night she took them to a dry thicket near by, and there among the crisp, dead leaves that would prevent an enemy's silent approach on foot, and under the interlacing briers that kept off all foes of the air, she cradled them in their feather-shingled nursery and rejoiced in the fullness of a mother's joy over the wee cuddling things that peeped in their sleep and snuggled so trustfully against her warm body.

2

The third day the chicks were much stronger on their feet. They no longer had to go around an acorn; they could even scramble over pine cones, and on the little tags that marked the places for their wings, were now to be seen blue rows of fat blood-quills.

Their start in life was a good mother, good legs, a few reliable instincts, and a germ of reason. It was instinct, that is, inherited habit, which taught them to hide at the word from their mother; it was instinct that taught them to follow her, but it was reason which made them keep under the shadow of her tail when the sun was smiting down, and from that day reason entered more and more into their expanding lives.

Next day the blood-quills had sprouted the tips of feathers. On the next, the feathers were well out, and a week later the whole family of down-clad babies were strong on the wing.

And yet not all — poor little Runtie had been sickly from the first. He bore his half-shell on his back for hours after he came out; he ran less and cheeped more than his brothers, and when one evening at the onset of a skunk the mother gave the word "Kwit, kwit" (Fly, fly), Runtie was left behind, and when she gathered her brood on the piney hill he was missing, and they saw him no more.

Meanwhile, their training had gone on. They knew that the finest grasshoppers abounded in the long grass by the brook; they knew that the currantbushes dropped fatness in the form of smooth, green worms; they knew that the dome of an ant-hill rising against the distant woods stood for a garner of plenty; they knew that strawberries, though not really insects, were almost as delicious; they knew that the huge denaid butterflies were good, safe game, if they could only catch them, and that a slab of bark dropping from the side of a rotten log was sure to abound in good things of many different kinds; and they had learned, also, that yellowjackets, mud-wasps, woolly worms, and hundred-leggers were better let alone.

It was now July, the Moon of Berries. The chicks had grown and flourished amazingly during this last month, and were now so large that in her efforts to cover them the mother was kept standing all night.

They took their daily dust-bath, but of late had changed to another higher on the hill. It was one in use by many different birds, and at first the mother disliked the idea of such a second-hand bath. But the dust was of such a fine, agreeable quality, and the children led the way with such enthusiasm, that she forgot her mistrust.

After a fortnight the little ones began to droop and she herself did not feel very well. They were always hungry, and though they ate enormously, they one and all grew thinner and thinner. The mother was the last to be affected. But when it came, it came as hard on her — a ravenous hunger, a feverish headache, and a wasting weakness. She never knew the cause. She could not know that the dust of the much-used dust-bath, that her true instinct taught her to mistrust at first, and now again to shun, was sown with parasitic worms, and that all of the family were infested.

No natural impulse is without a purpose. The mother-bird's knowledge of healing was only to follow natural impulse. The eager, feverish craving for something, she knew not what, led her to eat, or try, everything that looked eatable and to seek the coolest woods. And there she found a deadly sumach laden with its poison fruit. A month ago she would have passed it by, but now she tried the unattractive berries. The acrid burning juice seemed to answer some strange demand of her body; she ate and ate, and all her family joined in the strange feast of physic. No human doctor could have hit it better; it proved a biting, drastic purge, the dreadful secret foe was downed, the danger passed. But not for all — Nature, the old nurse, had come too late for two of them. The weakest, by inexorable law, dropped out. Enfeebled by the disease, the remedy was too severe for them. They drank and drank by the stream, and next morning did not move when the others followed the mother. Strange vengeance was theirs now, for a skunk the same that could have told where Runtie went, found and devoured their bodies and died of the poison they had eaten.

Seven little partridges now obeyed the mother's call. Their individual characters were early shown and now developed fast. The weaklings were gone, but there were still a fool and a lazy one. The mother could not help caring for some more than for others, and her favorite was the biggest, he who once sat on the yellow chip for concealment. He was not only the biggest, strongest, and handsomest of the brood, but best of all, the most obedient. His mother's warning "rrrrr" (danger) did not always keep the others from a risky path or a doubtful food, but obedience seemed natural to him, and he never failed to respond to her soft "K-reet" (Come), and of this obedience he reaped the reward, for his days were longest in the land.

August, the Molting Moon, went by; the young ones were now three parts grown. They knew just enough to think themselves wonderfully wise. When they were small it was necessary to sleep on the ground so their mother could shelter them, but now they were too big to need that, and the mother began to introduce grown-up ways of life. It was time to roost in the trees. The young weasels, foxes, skunks, and minks were beginning to run. The ground grew more dangerous each night, so at sundown Mother Partridge called "kreet", and flew into a thick, low tree.

The little ones followed, except one, an obstinate little fool who persisted in sleeping on the ground as heretofore. It was all right that time, but the next night his brothers were awakened by his cries. There was a slight scuffle, then stillness, broken only by a horrid sound of crunching bones and a smacking of lips. They peered down into the terrible darkness below, where the glint of two close-set eyes and a peculiar musty smell told them that a mink was the killer of their fool brother.

Six little partridges now sat in a row at night, with their mother in the middle, though it was not unusual for some little one with cold feet to perch on her back.

Their education went on, and about this time they were taught 'whirring.' A partridge can rise on the wing silently if it wishes, but whirring is so important at times that all are taught how and when to rise on thundering wings. Many ends are gained by the whirr. It warns all other partridges near that danger is at hand, it unnerves the gunner, or it fixes the foe's attention on the whirrer, while the others sneak off in silence, or by squatting, escape notice.

A partridge adage might well be 'foes and food for every moon.' September came, with seeds and grain in place of berries and ant-eggs, and gunners in place of skunks and minks.

The partridges knew well what a fox was, but had scarcely seen a dog. A fox they knew they could easily baffle by taking to a tree, but when in the Gunner Moon old Cuddy came prowling through the ravine with his bob-tailed yellow cur, the mother spied the dog and cried out, "Kwit! kwit!" (Fly, fly). Two of the brood thought it a pity their mother should lose her wits so easily over a fox, and were pleased to show their superior nerve by springing into a tree in spite of her earnestly repeated "Kwit! kwit!" and her example of speeding away on silent wings.

Meanwhile, the strange bob-tailed fox came under the tree and yapped and yapped at them. They were much amused at him and at their mother and brothers, so much so that they never noticed a rustling in the bushes till there was a loud Bang! bang! and down fell two bloody, flopping partridges, to be seized and mangled by the yellow cur until the gunner ran from the bushes and rescued the remains.

3

Cuddy lived in a wretched shanty near the Don, north of Toronto. His was what Greek philosophy would have demonstrated to be an ideal existence. He had no wealth, no taxes, no social pretensions, and no property to speak of. His life was made up of a very little work and a great deal of play, with as much outdoor life as he chose. He considered himself a true sportsman because he was 'fond o' huntin',' and 'took a sight o' comfort out of seein' the critters hit the mud' when his gun was fired. The neighbors called him a squatter, and looked on him merely as an anchored tramp. He shot and trapped the year round, and varied his game somewhat with the season perforce, but had been heard to remark he could tell the month by the 'taste o' the patndges,' if he didn't happen to know by the almanac. This, no doubt, showed keen observation, but was also unfortunate proof of something not so creditable. The lawful season for murdering partridges began September 15th, but there was nothing surprising in Cuddy's being out a fortnight ahead of time. Yet he managed to escape punishment year after year, and even contrived to pose in a newspaper interview as an interesting character.

He rarely shot on the wing, preferring to pot his birds, which was not easy to do when the leaves were on, and accounted for the brood in the third ravine going so long unharmed; but the near prospect of other gunners finding them now, had stirred him to go after 'a mess o' birds.' He had heard no roar of wings when the mother-bird led off her four survivors, so pocketed the two he had killed and returned to the shanty.

The little grouse thus learned that a dog is not a fox, and must be differently played; and an old lesson was yet more deeply graven — 'Obedience is long life.'

The rest of September was passed in keeping quietly out of the way of gunners as well as some old enemies. They still roosted on the long thin branches of the hardwood trees among the thickest leaves, which protected them from foes in the air; the height saved them from foes on the ground, and left them nothing to fear but coons, whose slow, heavy tread on the limber boughs never failed to give them timely warning. But the leaves were falling now every month its foes and its food. This was nut time, and it was owl time, too. Barred owls coming down from the north doubled or trebled the owl population. The nights were getting frosty and the coons less dangerous, so the mother changed the place of roosting to the thickest foliage of a hemlock-tree.

Only one of the brood disregarded the warning "Kreet, Kreet." He stuck to his swinging elm-bough, now nearly naked, and a great yellow-eyed owl bore him off before morning.

Mother and three young ones now were left, but they were as big as she was; indeed one, the eldest, he of the chip, was bigger. Their ruffs had begun to show. Just the tips, to tell what they would be like when grown, and not a little proud they were of them.

The ruff is to the partridge what the train is to the peacock — his chief beauty and his pride. A hen's ruff is black with a slight green gloss. A cock's is much larger and blacker and is glossed with more vivid bottle-green. Once in a while a partridge is born of unusual size and vigor, whose ruff is not only larger, but by a peculiar kind of intensification is of a deep coppery red, iridescent with violet, green, and gold. Such a bird is sure to be a wonder to all who know him, and the little one who had squatted on the chip, and had always done what he was told, developed before the Acorn Moon had changed, into all the glory of a gold and copper ruff—for this was Redruff, the famous partridge of the Don Valley.

4

One day late in the Acorn Moon, that is, about mid-October, as the grouse family were basking with full crops near a great pine log on the sunlit edge of the beaver-meadow, they heard the far-away bang of a gun, and Redruff, acting on some impulse from within, leaped on the log, strutted up and down a couple of times, then, yielding to the elation of the bright, clear, bracing air, he whirred his wings in loud defiance. Then, giving fuller vent to this expression of vigor, just as a colt frisks to show how well he feels, he whirred yet more loudly, until, unwittingly, he found himself drumming, and tickled with the discovery of his new power, thumped the air again and again till he filled the near woods with the loud tattoo of the fully grown cock-partridge. His brother and sister heard and looked on with admiration and surprise; so did his mother, but from that time she began to be a little afraid of him.

In early November comes the moon of a weird foe. By a strange law of nature, not wholly without parallel among mankind, all partridges go crazy in the November moon of their first year. They become possessed of a mad hankering to get away somewhere, it does not matter much where. And the wisest of them do all sorts of foolish things at this period. They go drifting, perhaps, at speed over the country by night, and are cut in two by wires, or dash into lighthouses, or locomotive headlights. Daylight finds them in all sorts of absurd places, in buildings, in open marshes, perched on telephone wires in a great city, or even on board of coasting vessels. The craze seems to be a relic of a bygone habit of migration, and it has at least one good effect, it breaks up the families and prevents the constant intermarrying which would surely be fatal to their race. It always takes the young badly their first year, and they may have it again the second fall, for it is very catching; but in the third season it is practically unknown.

Redruff's mother knew it was coming as soon as she saw the frost grapes blackening, and the maples shedding their crimson and gold. There was nothing to do but care for their health and keep them in the quietest part of the woods.

The first sign of it came when a flock of wild geese went honking southward overhead. The young ones had never before seen such long-necked hawks, and were afraid of them. But seeing that their mother had no fear, they took courage, and watched them with intense interest. Was it the wild, clanging cry that moved them, or was it solely the inner prompting then come to the surface? A strange longing to follow took possession of each of the young ones. They watched those arrowy trumpeters fading away to the south, and sought out higher perches to watch them farther yet, and from that time things were no more the same. The November moon was waxing, and when it was full, the November madness came.

The least vigorous of the flock were most affected. The little family was scattered. Redruff himself flew on several long erratic night journeys. The impulse took him southward, but there lay the boundless stretch of Lake Ontario, so he turned again, and the waning of the Mad Moon found him once more in the Mud Creek Glen, but absolutely alone.

5

Food grew scarce as winter wore on. Redruff clung to the old ravine and the piney sides of Taylor's Hill, but every month brought its food and its foes. The Mad Moon brought madness, solitude, and grapes; the Snow Moon came with rosehips; and the Stormy Moon brought browse of birch and silver storms that sheathed the woods in ice, and made it hard to keep one's perch while pulling off the frozen buds. Redruff's beak grew terribly worn with the work so that even when closed there was still an opening through behind the hook. But nature had prepared him for the slippery footing; his toes, so slim and trim in September, had sprouted rows of sharp, horny points, and these grew with the growing cold, till the first snow had found him fully equipped with snowshoes and ice-creepers. The cold weather had driven away most of the hawks and owls, and made it impossible for his four-footed enemies to approach unseen, so that things were nearly balanced.

His flight in search of food had daily led him farther on, till he had discovered and explored the Rosedale Creek, with its banks of silver-birch, and Castle Frank, with its grapes and rowan berries, as well as Chester woods, where Amelanchier and Virginia-creeper swung their fruit-bunches, and checkerberries glowed beneath the snow.

He soon found out that for some strange reason men with guns did not go within the high fence of Castle Frank. So among these scenes he lived his life, learning new places, new foods, and grew wiser and more beautiful every day.

He was quite alone so far as kindred were concerned, but that scarcely seemed a hardship. Whereever he went he could see the jolly chickadees scrambling merrily about, and he remembered the time when they had seemed such big, important creatures. They were the most absurdly cheerful things in the woods. Before the autumn was fairly over they had begun to sing their famous refrain, 'Spring Soon,' and kept it up with good heart more or less all through the winter's direst storms, till at length the waning of the Hunger Moon, our February, seemed really to lend some point to the ditty, and they redoubled their optimistic announcement to the world in an 'I-told-you-so' mood. Soon good support was found, for the sun gained strength and melted the snow from the southern slope of Castle Frank Hill, and exposed great banks of fragrant wintergreen, whose berries were a bounteous feast for Redruff, and, ending the hard work of pulling frozen browse, gave his bill the needed chance to grow into its proper shape again. Very soon the first bluebird came flying over and warbled as he flew 'The spring is coming.' The sun kept gaining, and early one day in the dark of the Wakening Moon of March there was a loud "Caw, caw," and old Silverspot, the king-crow, came swinging along from the south at the head of his troops and officially announced

"THE SPRING HAS COME."

All nature seemed to respond to this, the opening of the birds' New Year, and yet it was something within that chiefly seemed to move them. The chickadees went simply wild; they sang their "Spring now, spring now now-Spring now now," so persistently that one wondered how they found time to get a living.

And Redrulf felt it thrill him through and through. He sprang with joyous vigor on a stump and sent rolling down the little valley, again and again, a thundering "Thump, thump, thump, thunderrrrrrrr," that wakened dull echoes as it rolled, and voiced his gladness in the coming of the spring.

Away down the valley was Cuddy's shanty. He heard the drum-call on the still morning air and 'reckoned there was a cock patridge to git,' and came sneaking up the ravine with his gun. But Redruff skimmed away in silence, nor rested till once more in Mud Creek Glen. And there he mounted the very log where first he had drummed and rolled his loud tattoo again and again, till a small boy who had taken a short cut to the mill through the woods, ran home, badly scared, to tell his mother he was sure the Indians were on the war-path, for he heard their wardrums beating in the glen.

Why does a happy boy holla? Why does a lonesome youth sigh? They don't know any more than Redruff knew why every day now he mounted some dead log and thumped and thundered to the woods; then strutted and admired his gorgeous blazing ruffs as they flashed their jewels in the sunlight, and then thundered out again. Whence now came the strange wish for someone else to admire the plumes? And why had such a notion never come till the Pussywillow Moon?

"Thump, thump, thunder-r-r-r-r-r-rrrr"
"Thump, thump, thunder-r-r-r-r-r-rrrr"

he rumbled again and again.

Day after day he sought the favorite log, and a new beauty, a rose-red comb, grew out above each clear, keen eye, and the clumsy snowshoes were wholly shed from his feet. His ruff grew finer, his eye brighter, and his whole appearance splendid to behold, as he strutted and flashed in the sun. But — oh! he was so lonesome now.

Yet what could he do but blindly vent his hankering in this daily drum-parade, till on a day early in loveliest May, when the trilliums had fringed his log with silver stars, and he had drummed and longed, then drummed again, his keen ear caught a sound, a gentle footfall in the brush. He turned to a statue and watched; he knew he had been watched. Could it be possible? Yes! there it was — a form — another — a shy little lady grouse, now bashfully seeking to hide. In a moment he was by her side. His whole nature swamped by a new feeling — burnt up with thirst — a cooling spring in sight. And how he spread and flashed his proud array! How came he to know that that would please? He puffed his plumes and contrived to stand just right to catch the sun, and strutted and uttered a low, soft chuckle that must have been just as good as the 'sweet nothings' of another race, for clearly now her heart was won. Won, really, days ago, if only he had known. For full three days she had come at the loud tattoo and coyly admired him from afar, and felt a little piqued that he had not yet found her out, so close at hand. So it was not quite all mischance, perhaps, that little stamp that caught his ear. But now she meekly bowed her head with sweet, submissive grace the desert passed, the parch-burnt wanderer found the spring at last.

Oh, those were bright, glad days in the lovely glen of the unlovely name. The sun was never so bright, and the piney air was balmier sweet than dreams. And that great noble bird came daily on his log, sometimes with her and sometimes quite alone, and drummed for very joy of being alive. But why sometimes alone? Why not forever with his Brownie bride? Why should she stay to feast and play with him for hours, then take some stealthy chance to slip away and see him no more for hours or till next day, when his martial music from the log announced him restless for her quick return? There was a woodland mystery here he could not clear. Why should her stay with him grow daily less till it was down to minutes, and one day at last she never came at all. Nor the next, nor the next, and Redruff, wild, careered on lightning wing and drummed on the old log, then away upstream on another log, and skimmed the hill to another ravine to drum and drum. But on the fourth day, when he came and loudly called her, as of old, at their earliest tryst, he heard a sound in the bushes, as at first, and there was his missing Brownie bride with ten little peeping partridges following after.

Redruff skimmed to her side, terribly frightening the bright-eyed downlings, and was just a little dashed to find the brood with claims far stronger than his own. But he soon accepted the change, and thenceforth joined himself to the brood, caring for them as his father never had for him.

<h2 style="text-align:center">6</h2>

Good fathers are rare in the grouse world. The mother-grouse builds her nest and hatches out her young without help. She even hides the place of the nest from the father and meets him only at the drum-log and the feeding-ground, or perhaps the dusting-place, which is the clubhouse of the grouse kind.

When Brownie's little ones came out they had filled her every thought, even to the forgetting of their splendid father. But on the third day, when they were strong enough, she had taken them with her at the father's call.

Some fathers take no interest in their little ones, but Redruff joined at once to help Brownie in the task of rearing the brood. They had learned to eat and drink just as their father had learned long ago, and could toddle along, with their mother leading the way, while the father ranged near by or followed far behind.

The very next day, as they went from the hill-side down toward the creek in a somewhat drawn-out string, like beads with a big one at each end, a red squirrel, peeping around a pine-trunk watched the procession of downlings with the Runtie straggling far in the rear. Redruff, yards behind, preening his feathers on a high log, had escaped the eye of the squirrel, whose strange perverted thirst for birdling blood was roused at what seemed so fair a chance. With murderous intent to cut off the hindmost straggler, he made a dash. Brownie could not have seen him until too late, but Redruff did. He flew for that red-haired cutthroat; his weapons were his fists, that is, the knob-joints of the wings, and what a blow he could strike! At the first onset he struck the squirrel square on the end of the nose, his weakest spot, and sent him reeling; he staggered and wriggled into a brush-pile, where he had expected to carry the little grouse, and there lay gasping with red drops trickling down his wicked snout. The partridges left him lying there, and what became of him they never knew, but he troubled them no more.

The family went on toward the water, but a cow had left deep tracks in the sandy loam, and into one of these fell one of the chicks and peeped in dire distress when he found he could not get out.

This was a fix. Neither old one seemed to know what to do, but as they trampled vainly round the edge, the sandy bank caved in, and, running down, formed a long slope, up which the young one ran and rejoined his brothers under the broad veranda of their mother's tail.

Brownie was a bright little mother, of small stature, but keen of wit and sense, and was, night and day, alert to care for her darling chicks. How proudly she stepped and clucked through the arching woods with her daintybrood behind her; how she strained her little brown tail almost to a halfcircle to give them a broader shade, and never flinched at sight of any foe, but held ready to fight or fly, whichever seemed the best for her little ones.

Before the chicks could fly they had a meeting with old Cuddy; though it was June, he was out with his gun. Up the third ravine he went, and Tike, his dog, ranging ahead, came so dangerously near the Brownie brood that Redruff ran to meet him, and by the old but never failing trick led him on a foolish chase away back down the valley of the Don.

But Cuddy, as it chanced, came right along, straight for the brood, and Brownie, giving the signal to the children, "Krrr, krrr" (Hide, hide), ran to lead the man away just as her mate had led the dog. Full of a mother's devoted love, and skilled in the learning of the woods, she ran in silence till quite near, then sprang with a roar of wings right in his face, and tumbling on the leaves she shammed a lameness that for a moment deceived the poacher. But when she dragged one wing and whined about his feet, then slowly crawled away, he knew just what it meant — that it was all a trick to lead him from her brood, and he struck at her a savage blow; but little Brownie was quick, she avoided the blow and limped behind a sapling, there to beat herself upon the leaves again in sore distress, and seem so lame that Cuddy made another try to strike her down with a stick. But she moved in time to balk him, and bravely, steadfast still to lead him from her helpless little ones, she flung herself before him and beat her gentle breast upon the ground, and moaned as though begging for mercy. And Cuddy, failing again to strike her, raised his gun, and firing charge enough to kill a bear, he blew poor brave, devoted Brownie into quivering, bloody rags.

This gunner brute knew the young must be hiding near, so looked about to find them. But no one moved or peeped. He saw not one, but as he tramped about with heedless, hateful feet, he crossed and crossed again their hiding-ground, and more than one of the silent little sufferers he trampled to death, and neither knew nor cared.

Redruff had taken the yellow brute away off downstream, and now returned to where he left his mate. The murderer had gone, taking her remains, to be thrown to the dog. Redruff sought about and found the bloody spot with feathers, Brownie's feathers, scattered around, and now he knew the meaning of that shot.

Who can tell what his horror and his mourning were? The outward signs were few, some minutes dumbly gazing at the place with downcast, draggled look, and then a change at the thought of their helpless brood. Back to the hiding-place he went, and called the well-known "Kreet, kreet." Did every grave give up its little inmate at the magic word? No, barely more than half; six little balls of down unveiled their lustrous eyes, and, rising, ran to meet him, but four feathered little bodies had found their graves indeed. Redruff called again and again, till he was sure that all who could respond had come, then led them from that dreadful place, far, far away up-stream, where barb-wire fences and bramble thickets were found to offer a less grateful, but more reliable, shelter.

Here the brood grew and were trained by their father just as his mother had trained him; though wider knowledge and experience gave him many advantages. He knew so well the country round and all the feeding-grounds, and how to meet the ills that harass partridge-life, that the summer passed and not a chick was lost. They grew and flourished, and when the Gunner Moon arrived they were a fine family of six grown-up grouse with Redruff, splendid in his gleaming copper feathers, at their head. He had ceased to drum during the summer after the loss of Brownie, but drumming is to the partridge what singing is to the lark; while it is his love-song, it is also an expression of exuberance born of health, and when the molt was over and September food and weather had renewed his splendid plumes and braced him up again, his spirits revived, and finding himself one day near the old log he mounted impulsively, and drummed again and again.

From that time he often drummed, while his children sat around, or one who showed his father's blood would mount some nearby stump or stone, and beat the air in the loud tattoo.

The black grapes and the Mad Moon now came on. But Redruff's brood were of a vigorous stock; their robust health meant robust wits, and though they got the craze, it passed within a week and only three had flown away for good.

Redruff, with his remaining three, was living in the glen when the snow came. It was light, flaky snow, and as the weather was not very cold, the family squatted for the night under the low, flat boughs of a cedar-tree. But next day the storm continued, it grew colder, and the drifts piled up all day. At night, the snow-fall ceased, but the frost grew harder still, so Redruff, leading the family to a birch-tree above a deep drift, dived into the snow, and the others did the same. Then into the holes the wind blew the loose snow — their pure white bed-clothes, and thus tucked in they slept in comfort, for the snow is a warm wrap, and the air passes through it easily enough for breathing. Next morning each partridge found a solid wall of ice before him from his frozen breath, but easily turned to one side and rose on the wing at Redruff's morning "Kreet, kreet, kwit." (Come children, come children, fly.)

This was the first night for them in a snowdrift, though it was an old story to Redruff, and next night they merrily dived again into bed, and the north wind tucked them in as before. But a change of weather was brewing. The night wind veered to the east. A fall of heavy flakes gave place to sleet, and that to silver rain. The whole wide world was sheathed in ice, and when the grouse awoke to quit their beds, they found themselves sealed in with a great cruel sheet of edgeless ice.

The deeper snow was still quite soft, and Redruff bored his way to the top, but there the hard, white sheet defied his strength. Hammer and struggle as he might he could make no impression, and only bruised his wings and head. His life had been made up of keen joys and dull hardships, with frequent sudden desperate straits, but this seemed the hardest brunt of all, as the slow hours wore on and found him weakening with his struggles, but no nearer to freedom. He could hear the struggling of his family, too, or sometimes heard them calling to him for help with their long-drawn plaintive "p-e-e-e-e-e-t-e, p-e-e-e-e-e-t-e."

They were hidden from many of their enemies, but not from the pangs of hunger, and when the night came down the weary prisoners, worn out with hunger and useless toil, grew quiet in despair. At first they had been afraid the fox would come and find them imprisoned there at his mercy, but as the second night went slowly by they no longer cared, and even wished he would come and break the crusted snow, and so give them at least a fighting chance for life.

But when the fox really did come padding over the frozen drift, the deep-laid love of life revived, and they crouched in utter stillness till he passed. The second day was one of driving storm. The north wind sent his snow-horses, hissing and careering over the white earth, tossing and curling their white manes and kicking up more snow as they dashed on. The long, hard grinding of the granular snow seemed to be thinning the snow-crust, for though far from dark below, it kept on growing lighter. Redruff had pecked and pecked at the under side all day, till his head ached and his bill was wearing blunt, but when the sun went down he seemed as far as ever from escape. The night passed like the others, except no fox went trotting overhead. In the morning he renewed his pecking, though now with scarcely any force, and the voices or struggles of the others were no more heard. As the daylight grew stronger he could see that his long efforts had made a brighter spot above him in the snow, and he continued feebly peeking. Outside, the stormhorses kept on trampling all day, the crust was really growing thin under their heels, and late that afternoon his bill went through into the open air. New life came with this gain, and he pecked away, till just before the sun went down he had made a hole that his head, his neck, and his ever-beautiful ruffs could pass. His great broad shoulders were too large, but he could now strike downward, which gave him fourfold force; the snow-crust crumbled quickly, and in a little while he sprang from his icy prison once more free. But the young ones! Redruff flew to the nearest bank, hastily gathered a few red hips to stay his gnawing hunger, then returned to the prisondrift and clucked and stamped. He got only one reply, a feeble "peete, peete," and scratching with his sharp claws on the thinned granular sheet he soon broke through, and Graytail feebly crawled out of the hole. But that was all; the others, scattered he could not tell where in the drift, made no reply, gave no sign of life, and he was forced to leave them. When the snow melted in the spring their bodies came to view, skin, bones, and feathers — nothing more.

7

It was long before Redruff and Graytail fully recovered, but food and rest in plenty are sure curealls, and a bright clear day in midwinter had the usual effect of setting the vigorous Redruff to drumming on the log. Was it the drumming, or the telltale tracks of their snowshoes on the omnipresent snow, that betrayed them to Cuddy? He came prowling again and again up the ravine, with dog and gun, intent to hunt the partridges down. They knew him of old, and he was coming now to know them well. That great copper-ruff cock was becoming famous up and down the valley. During the Gunner Moon many a one had tried to end his splendid life, just as a worthless wretch of old sought fame by burning the Ephesian wonder of the world. But Redruff was deep in woodcraft. He knew just where to hide, and when to rise on silent wing, and when to squat till overstepped, then rise on thunder wing within a yard to shield himself at once behind some mighty tree-trunk and speed away.

But Cuddy never ceased to follow with his gun that red-ruffed cock; many a long snapshot he tried, but somehow always found a tree, a bank, or some safe shield between, and Redruff lived and throve and drummed.

When the Snow Moon came he moved with Graytail to the Castle Frank woods, where food was plenty as well as grand old trees. There was in particular, on the east slope among the creeping hemlocks, a splendid pine. It was six feet through, and its first branches began at the tops of the other trees. Its top in summer-time was a famous resort for the bluejay and his bride. Here, far beyond the reach of shot, in warm spring days the jay would sing and dance before his mate, spread his bright blue plumes and warble the sweetest fairyland music, so sweet and soft that few hear it but the one for whom it is meant, and books know nothing at all about it.

This great pine had an especial interest for Redruff, now living near with his remaining young one, but its base, not its far-away crown, concerned him. All around were low, creeping hemlocks, and among them the partridgevine and the wintergreen grew, and the sweet black acorns could be scratched from under the snow. There was no better feeding-ground, for when that insatiable gunner came on them there it was easy to run low among the hemlock to the great pine, then rise with a derisive whirr behind its bulk, and keeping the huge trunk in line with the deadly gun, skim off in safety. A dozen times at least the pine had saved them during the lawful murder season, and here it was that Cuddy, knowing their feeding habits, laid a new trap. Under the bank he sneaked and watched in ambush while an accomplice went around the Sugar Loaf to drive the birds. He came trampling through the low thicket where Redruff and Graytail were feeding, and long before the gunner was dangerously near Redruff gave a low warning "rrr-rrr" (danger) and walked quickly toward the great pine in case they had to rise.

Graytail was some distance up the hill, and suddenly caught sight of a new foe close at hand, the yellow cur, coming right on. Redruff, much farther off, could not see him for the bushes, and Graytail became greatly alarmed.

"Kwit, kwit" (Fly, fly), she cried, running down the hill for a start. "Kreet, k-r-r-r" (This way, hide), cried the cooler Redruff, for he saw that now the man with the gun was getting in range. He gained the great trunk, and behind it, as he paused a moment to call earnestly to Graytail, "This way, this way," he heard a slight noise under the bank before him that betrayed the ambush, then there was a terrified cry from Graytail as the dog sprang at her, she rose in air and skimmed behind the shielding trunk, away from the gunner in the open, right into the power of the miserable wretch under the bank.

Whirr, and up she went, a beautiful, sentient, noble being.

Bang, and down she fell — battered and bleeding, to gasp her life out and to lie, mere carrion in the snow.

It was a perilous place for Redruff. There was no chance for a safe rise, so he squatted low. The dog came within ten feet of him, and the stranger, coming across to Cuddy, passed at five feet, but he never moved till a chance came to slip behind the great trunk away from both. Then he safely rose and flew to the lonely glen by Taylor's Hill.

One by one the deadly cruel gun had stricken his near ones down, till now, once more, he was alone. The Snow Moon slowly passed with many a narrow escape, and Redruff, now known to be the only survivor of his kind, was relentlessly pursued, and grew wilder every day.

It seemed, at length, a waste of time to follow him with a gun, so when the snow was deepest, and food scarcest, Cuddy hatched a new plot. Right across the feeding-ground, almost the only good one now in the Stormy Moon, he set a row of snares. A cottontail rabbit, an old friend, cut several of these with his sharp teeth, but some remained, and Redruff, watching a far-off speck that might turn out a hawk, trod right in one of them, and in an instant was jerked into the air to dangle by one foot.

Have the wild things no moral or legal rights? What right has man to inflict such long and fearful agony on a fellow-creature, simply because that creature does not speak his language? All that day with growing, racking pains, poor Redruff hung and beat his great, strong wings in help-less struggles to be free. All day, all night, with growing torture, until he only longed for death. But no one came. The morning broke, the day wore on, and still he hung there, slowly dying; his very strength a curse.

The second night crawled slowly down, and when, in the dawdling hours of darkness, a great Horned owl, drawn by the feeble flutter of a dying wing, cut short the pain, the deed was wholly kind.

The wind blew down the valley from the north. The snow-horses went racing over the wrinkled ice, over the Don Flats, and over the marsh toward the lake, white, for they were driven snow, but on them, scat-tered dark, were riding plushy fragments of partridge ruffs — the famous rainbow ruffs. And they rode on the winter wind that night, away and away to the south, over the dark and boisterous lake, as they rode in the gloom of his Mad Moon flight, riding and riding on till they were engulfed, the last trace of the last of the Don Valley race.

For now no partridge comes to Castle Frank. Its woodbirds miss the martial spring salute, and in Mud Creek Ravine the old pine drumlog, since unused, has rotted in silence away.

Notes on the Authors

HANS CHRISTIAN ANDERSEN (1805–1875). Born in Odense, Denmark, his tales were published in Britain in 1846 and were extremely popular. His "rags-to-riches" success was built on his talent as a teller of tales, most of which came from his working class background.

MARIUS BARBEAU (1883–1969). Born in Quebec, a Rhodes Scholar, was in 1911 made an anthropologist to the National Museum of Canada until he retired in 1949. Among his volumes of legends, stories, and songs is *The Indian Speaks* (1943), from which the tales here are taken. A prolific collector, Barbeau is credited as the founder of Canadian folklore studies.

JAKOB GRIMM (1785–1863) and WILHELM GRIMM (1786–1859). Born in Hanau, Germany, dedicated to the work of collecting and editing the folk tales of their country. Their tales, *Kinder- und Haus-Märchen*, were published in three volumes (1812, 1815, 1822).

JOEL CHANDLER HARRIS (1848–1908). Born in Eatonton, Georgia, a journalist by profession, published *Uncle Remus: His Songs and Sayings* in 1880. The widespread popularity of this volume led to eight others in Harris's life-time. Theodore Roosevelt praised Harris's work for the "blotting out of sectional antagonism".

RUDYARD KIPLING (1865–1936). Born in Bombay, returned to England for school in 1871, then returned to India for a career in journalism in 1882. The first Englishman to receive the Nobel Prize for Literature (1907).

CHARLES PERRAULT (1628–1703). Born in Paris, published in 1697 his *Histoires ou Contes du temps passé — avec des Moralitez*, containing eight of our most popular fairy tales.

ERNEST THOMPSON SETON (1860–1946). Born in England, Seton moved to Canada in 1866, studied at the Ontario College of Art, and wrote around forty volumes on various topics associated with "nature" and natural history. He was an avid reader of Cooper, an outspoken admirer of the North American Indian, and Chief of the Boy Scouts of America. His animal stories, he believed, are true and have tragic endings because the lives of wild animals end tragically.

OSCAR WILDE (1854–1900). Born in Dublin, his short stories were published between 1887 and 1891. Imprisoned in 1895 for homosexual conduct, Wilde died in obscurity in Paris in 1900.

Selected Texts for Further Study

Barchilon, Jacques and Peter Flinders. *Charles Perrault*. Boston: Twayne Publishers, 1981.

Bettelheim, Bruno. *The Uses of Enchantment: The Meaning and Importance of Fairy Tales*. New York: Alfred Knopf, 1976.

Brewer, Derek. *Symbolic Stories: Traditional Narratives of the Family Drama in English Literature*. Totawa, NJ: Rowman and Littlefield, 1980.

Dundes, Alan, ed. *Cinderella: A Casebook*. Madison: University of Wisconsin Press, 1988.

Ellis, John M. *One Fairy Story Too Many: The Brothers Grimm and Their Tales*. Chicago: University of Chicago Press, 1983.

Franz, Marie Louise von. *An Introduction to The Psychology of Fairy Tales*. 3rd. ed. Zurich: Spring Publications, 1975.

——— . *Individuation in Fairy Tales*. Zurich: Spring Publications, 1977.

——— . *Problems of the Feminine in Fairy Tales*. Irving, Texas: Spring Publications, 1979.

Gronbech, Bo. *Hans Christian Andersen*. Boston: Twayne Publishers, 1980.

Hearne, Betsy G., ed. *Beauty and the Beast: Visions and Revisions of an Old Tale*. Chicago: University of Chicago Press, 1989.

Kamenetsky, Christa. *The Brothers Grimm and Their Critics: Folk Tales and the Quest for Meaning*. Athens: Ohio University Press, 1992.

Kolbenschlag. Madonna. *Kiss Sleeping Beauty Goodbye*. Garden City, NY: Doubleday, 1979.

Lane, Marcia. *Picturing the Rose: A Way of Looking at Fairy Tales*. New York: H.W. Wilson Co., 1994.

Lang, Andrew, ed. *The Blue Fairy Book*. New York: Airmont Publishing Co., 1969.

Lederer, Wolfgang. *The Kiss of the Snow Queen: Hans Christian Andersen and Man's Redemption by Woman*. Berkeley: University of California Press, 1986.

Lüthi, Max. *Once Upon a Time: On the Nature of Fairy Tales*. Translated by Lee Chadeayne and Paul Gottwald. New York: Frederick Ungar, 1970.

McGlathery, James M. *Fairy Tale Romance: The Grimms, Basile and Perrault*. Urbana: University of Illinois Press, 1991.

Opie, Iona and Peter, eds. *The Classic Fairy Tale*. London: Oxford University Press, 1974.

Propp, Vladimir. *The Morphology of the Folktale*. Austin: University of Texas Press, 1968.

Sale, Roger. *Fairy Tales and After: From Snow White to E.B. White*. Cambridge, Mass.: Harvard University Press, 1978.

Tatar, Maria M. *Off With Their Heads!: Fairy Tales and the Culture of Childhood*. Princeton, NJ: Princeton University Press, 1992.

——. *The Hard Facts of the Grimms' Fairy Tales*. Princeton, NJ: Princeton University Press, 1987.

Warner, Marina. *From the Beast to the Blonde*. London: Chatto and Windus, 1994.

Wilson, Anne. *Traditional Romance and Tale: How Stories Mean*. Ipswich: D.S. Brewer, Rowman and Littlefield, 1976.

Zipes, Jack D. *Breaking the Magic Spell: Radical Theories of Folk and Fairy Tale*. Austin: University of Texas Press, 1979.

——. *Fairy Tales and the Art of Subversion: The Classic Genre for Children and the Process of Civilization*. London: Heinemann, 1983.

——. *The Brothers Grimm: From Enchanted Forests to the Modern World*. New York: Routledge, 1988.

——. *The Trials and Tribulations of Little Red Riding Hood: Versions of the Tale in Sociocultural Context*. South Hadley, Mass.: Bergin and Garvey, 1983.

• Cap-Saint-Ignace
• Sainte-Marie (Beauce)
Québec, Canada
1996

«L'IMPRIMEUR»